GIVEN

HIGHEST BIDDER

LAUREN LANDISH

WILLOW WINTERS

Photography by
ERIC BATTERSHELL
Illustrated by
COVERLUV

Copyright © 2017 by Lauren Landish & Willow Winters.

All rights reserved.

No part of this book may be reproduced in any form or by any electronic or mechanical means, including information storage and retrieval systems, without written permission from the author, except for the use of brief quotations in a book review.

This book is a work of fiction. Names, characters, places, and incidents are either the product of the author's imagination or are used fictitiously, and any resemblance to actual persons, living or dead, events, or locales is entirely coincidental.

The following story contains mature themes, strong language and sexual situations. It is intended for mature readers.

All characters are 18+ years of age and all sexual acts are consensual.

GIVEN: HIGHEST BIDDER

BY LAUREN LANDISH & WILLOW WINTERS

I knew she'd ruin me. But I wanted her anyway.

I was born into wealth and my name comes with a reputation.
One I've upheld and leveraged for power.
Now everyone owes me and I plan to keep it that way.

Until she's offered to me. My sweetheart. Only for a single month to repay a debt.
Her tempting curves call to me and beg me to risk it all.

I shouldn't take her, I shouldn't even consider his offer.

Women like her bring men to their knees.

But there's something in her baby blues. They're haunted by what lies behind them.
She sees through me, leaving me nowhere to hide.

I knew taking her would destroy me, but it only took one taste.

Now I'm addicted. And I'm not giving her back.

❄

Want more? Join our mailing list to receive bonus deleted scenes!

Need more of the Highest Bidder Series? Check out the other books:
Book 1: Bought
Book 2: Sold
Book 3: Owned

PROLOGUE

ZANDER

Both of my hands tremble, and the adrenaline pumping in my blood makes my muscles coil, ready to fight. I grip the edge of the dresser to keep my body upright. I only need to breathe. A long and slow exhale leaves me, lowering my tense shoulders. I crack my neck before looking over my shoulder at her. *My sweetheart.*

I've never run from anything in my life. And I'm not about to start now.

But I should have run from *her*. I knew I should have walked away when I first laid eyes on her.

She's destroyed my control. Ruined my reputation. She'll be the end of me, I know it.

Her soft moans of pain from across the bedroom call to me. She's so beautifully broken. She *needs* me.

I took it too far, and I can't take it back.

They'll come for me. I'm certain the cops will be here

soon. I'm guilty, and I have no one to blame. The evidence is all right here, and I can't deny a damn thing.

For the first time in my life, I don't see a way out.

There's no one I can turn to. No one who owes me who can make this right.

But I can't stop wanting her. She's gotten under my skin. And I won't stop fighting for her.

Never.

"Zander," she says, and her small voice is choked. Her brow is pinched as her head thrashes from side to side and the doctor works on the deep lashes on her back. Agony rises through my chest and stiffens my body. My eyes burn and my throat closes as I try to breathe.

She's stripped to the waist, lying face down on the bed, her bottom half barely covered by a thin white sheet to keep the doctor's prying eyes from seeing even more of her.

I know what he thinks. What they all think since I took her.

I don't give a fuck. I pay him well to turn a blind eye, and that's exactly what he'll do. It's what they all do. They only want the money, and they'll do anything for it.

But not her.

The plush rug softens my heavy footsteps as I cross the master bedroom and walk to her. She lifts her head as I come closer, but the moment she does, she winces and sucks in a reluctant breath through clenched teeth.

I'm quick to gentle my hand on her shoulder, keeping my contact confined to the small area of soft skin without any wounds. "Don't move," I say, and my voice is low, admonishing even. I hate myself. I'm so devoid of the ability to comfort that I can't even speak softly to her when she's . . . like this.

"I'm sorry," Arianna says quietly, her voice muffled from the mattress.

A chill runs over every inch of my skin. She has no reason to apologize to me. She never did anything wrong. Not since the first moment this started.

I swallow thickly, and the lump forming in my throat feels as though it scratches the tender skin on the way down. "It's all right." I try to soften my voice and put as much warmth into it as possible. I pet her hair with soothing strokes.

"I never should have left you," Arianna replies, her words coming out slow and full of genuine remorse.

She shouldn't have. This wouldn't have happened if she'd just listened. If she'd *trusted* me.

But it's my fault. Not hers.

"It's going to be all right," I say softly, crouching down so my eyes are level with hers. It's a lie. It's not going to be all right. I'm damn sure of that single truth. Everything is fucked.

But I'll tell her whatever she needs to hear.

I can't lose her.

I press my lips to hers, my hand cupping her jaw and my thumb rubbing comforting circles on her soft skin.

"Is it going to be okay?" she whispers against my lips. It's only when I open my eyes and see that hers are still closed with tears running freely down her reddened cheeks that my heart shatters.

I wish I could tell her I'll take care of everything.

But it's not okay. And I can't fix this.

I know I shouldn't, but lying comes so easily to me. "Everything's going to be fine," I tell her. Her long lashes flutter and her gorgeous green eyes open to look back at me. So much raw vulnerability and something else are clearly evident in her gaze. Something that should push me away.

I didn't even want to take her when she was first given to me. I should have refused.

Maybe even then, I recognized what she would do to me. How she would change who I am and destroy everything I've worked for. When they put me behind bars, they'll figure out everything. The corruption, the money, all the lies.

Even knowing that, I wouldn't hesitate to take her if I had the chance to do it all over again. My hand clenches into a fist, firming my resolve. Even if I couldn't change a damn thing, I'd still accept that sick fuck's offer.

She was given to me.

Now she's *mine*.

CHAPTER 1

ZANDER

I clasp my hands behind my back, staring out of the floor-to-ceiling window in my office. It's on the top floor of Penn Square, one of the three tallest skyscrapers in the city. My fingers run along the cold metal of my Tag Heuer watch as I let my gaze fall to the world beneath me. My shoulders are squared and the rush of the city flows easily through my blood.

This is where I thrive, where I make the deals that run this city.

"Are you listening to me?" my father's voice spills from the speaker on my desk, and the corners of my lips turn up into a smirk.

"I am," I answer easily with an air of confidence I learned from him.

"You never should have accepted." His words are sharp and firm. But he's right.

A heavy sigh leaves me as my eyes narrow at the park

directly beneath the building. Although my blood chills at my father's words, I ignore him, cracking my knuckles and continuing to watch the specks of people moving about.

I'm the one who kept our family name from falling. We were going bankrupt because of *his* bad investments and trusting the wrong people. My teeth grind as I clench my jaw. Yes, I fucked up, but not nearly as much as he has. It's been almost ten fucking years of me rising to the top and carrying our legacy with me, creating a pristine reputation in the eyes of the community and business elites. I've also worked hard to create one of fear for those who run the underside of this city.

There are many men with power, but they all owe someone . . . and I happen to be that someone. My father's voice drones on as I move my gaze toward the streets. My father's still admonishing me for a single mistake.

A bad investment named Daniel Brooks.

That dumb fuck owes me a lot of money, more money than he should.

He knew how much debt he had, and he still gambled away my money. He thinks I don't know . . . I know *everything*. I was the first to know when the sum left his account and wasn't directly passed to mine.

This happens from time to time. *Everyone* owes me, and that's how I like it. It's only a matter of time before something gets between me and the money they owe me.

I don't care. I always come out on top, and that's what matters. Money isn't power. It's leverage. Being owed is power. True power. And that's what I want. It's what I have. But right now, Brooks isn't an asset, and I have no way of knowing just how he's going to pay me the almost half-million I'm due. It's not the largest sum, but it's a deal that was public. A debt that many are aware of, and therefore, it must be paid.

"Did you hear me?" My father's voice is low as I turn from the city to face my hard maple desk, my eyes focused and narrowed on the black corded phone that came with this office. It's at odds with the modern touches, but the line is traceable and I've been able to use that to my advantage more than a time or two.

"I did," I answer, although I'd rather hang up the phone altogether. I don't wait for him to reply.

"Brooks owes me more than what's excusable. More than he's worth." I take my seat, leaning back and propping up my feet on the long, sleek desk.

"You can't allow him to get away with it." My father speaks with authority.

Brooks may be a high-up executive and think he's untouchable, but the alcoholic, gambling degenerate is going to give me my money one way or the other. And then I'm done with him. I have enough pull to bury him if I want. I tap my fingers on the hard wood top, debating. The *rap, rap, rap* echoes rhythmically and calms me slightly.

I could destroy him slowly. Cripple him financially and embarrass him in every way possible. But few would know why, and he's too pathetic to waste that much time and effort on. No, I'll just take my money and be through with him. He'll hang himself on his own.

My eyes lift to the office door as a solid knock rebounds through the large space.

"Come in," I call out as my back settles against the leather desk chair, but my fingers never stop tapping on the desk as I wait for the door to open.

Charles walks in with a mask of indifference. I'm used to it. When I first met him all those years ago at boarding school, I thought there was something more behind his dark eyes. But now I know the truth—the only emotion I've ever seen reflected in his eyes is anger. It's that, or nothing. And I prefer nothing to his temper.

With short pitch-black hair and eyes to match, Charles is just as lethal as he looks. He didn't grow up with the lifestyle I'm accustomed to, but I made sure to make friends with him. It's been mutually beneficial.

I nod toward the phone before he has a chance to speak. Sharing a glance, he quietly shuts the door behind him, a soft *click* the only sound in my office.

"I'm going to have to call you back." I lean forward, speaking into the phone and preparing to hang up, knowing damn well that I won't return the phone call. There's nothing to discuss. He'll see me at the next social event, and until then, the only thing he'll give me is shit over this debt.

Charles is silent as he takes a seat across from me.

Placing an elbow on the arm of the chair, he stares back at me with his finger resting on his bottom lip.

Large black and white photos of the nighttime skyline decorate the wall behind him. The furnishings in my office are entirely black and white, with the walls painted a light grey. To an observer, my office may seem as if it's a minimalist and masculine design. And that's true, but more importantly, it suits me. Cold and simple. No room for bullshit.

I didn't even want the fucking blown-up photos, but I needed something to make the room seem . . . normal. Complete, even.

"We have a problem," Charles finally says after I've hung up the phone.

I may be deceptive. Born with a silver spoon in my mouth, I come off as playful and charming. They don't see me coming. And most of my clients never have a problem with me. The legal ones, anyway. It's a handshake and a smile, an exchange of money and profit. Those are ninety percent of my interactions. But the other ten percent, well, that's where Charles comes in. I can't get my hands dirty. My reputation is everything.

He doesn't attend the social galas and business openings. He doesn't give a fuck about rubbing elbows and being seen with the right people. He meets his clients in back alleys. As far as anyone's concerned, he's an associate.

Everyone in my life is just an associate. And that's never going to change.

"And what's that?" I ask him as my lips kick up into a

charming smile. It's always there. Even though it doesn't affect Charles, I can't help the false expression. I've learned to play this role. It pays me well.

"Brooks is a problem," he states and leans forward in his seat, grabbing a paperweight off my desk. It's a small slate cube, heavy with sharp edges. He runs his finger down one side.

Although he's not a threat to me, I can only imagine what he'd do with a weapon like that. I roll my eyes at what he just said and stretch my neck to look out of the large windows again as the sun sets behind us, darkening the room. I can't take another person telling me I've fucked up. I get it. I need someone to offer me a solution to fix it, not tell me the obvious.

"No shit," I say, waiting for his eyes to meet mine. It only takes a moment, and his movements stop.

"Are we offing him?" he asks me.

My blood turns cold, sending a biting wave through every inch of my body. It takes its time, slowly coursing through my veins. I don't take death lightly. Ending someone's life isn't as easy for me as it is for Charles. He grew up around it, made a career of it. Killing is simply a way of life for him. They all have it coming and for good reason, but he's quick to take it that far.

I break the hold his dark eyes have on mine and stare at the large clock on the left-hand wall. It's simple and modern, so there aren't any marks on it. It's just a large white circle with contrasting black hands. The second hand sweeps by, rhythmically and perfectly. There's no sound, but I can only imagine the soft *tick, tick, tick* in sync with my own heartbeat.

I click my tongue, feeling the smile fade for a moment before turning my attention back to Charles.

"Who did he give it to?" I ask him. Brooks had the money in his account. I know for a fact what Danny Brooks was worth when I loaned him the investment. It should have been a good return, had he done what he was supposed to do.

"A bookie," Charles answers in a rough, deep voice, setting the slate paperweight back down at my desk.

A huff of a humorless laugh rumbles up my chest.

"I'm guessing he thinks the bookie breaking his legs is worse than what you would have done to him," Charles adds and then cracks his neck and settles easily into his seat. He's probably right. Most of these men who work with contracts think I'd settle a dispute using the legal system.

I'm sure Brooks thinks I'll sue him. But that takes so much time and sets a poor example. It would tarnish my spotless reputation as well. I don't set foot into courtrooms. I'm not interested in a lawsuit or having anything in the paper.

When someone doesn't pay me, I make sure I get more than my money's worth of retribution. I think back to the dozens of men who have tried to get away from me and their debts in the past. They can't run though. They can't hide behind the law or in the shadows. *I own both.*

"So, what are you going to do?" Charles asks me, pulling me back to the present.

I sit up in my seat and lean closer to him, feeling that slick smile on my face. My blood heats and the resulting adrenaline fuels me. I speak slowly but firmly, staring hard into Charles's unforgiving stare as I say, "I want to know everything about Danny Brooks."

CHAPTER 2

ARIANNA

"They had rabbits, dildos, and pulsators," Natalie shamelessly continues as she sets down her paintbrush in the cup of now-dirty water that sits between us. She's got an asymmetric grin on her face as she rises from her seat to step back and survey her handiwork. "It was *awesome*," she says, and the smile doesn't fade as she stares at her canvas.

I stop my brush mid-stroke to look at her, arching a questioning eyebrow. Even dressed in pale blue overalls with old paint stains all over them, Natalie looks beautiful. She has the kind of natural beauty that comes equipped with confidence. Her dark brown hair cut in a short side bob sways as she crosses her arms and nods her head, and her large brown eyes widen as she steps forward and smudges a small spot on her canvas with her finger. The smile only fades for a moment until she's satisfied with the adjustment.

She lets out an easy sigh and her eyes sparkle as she meets my stare. I force a small smile back but avoid her gaze as I take in my own canvas. I've been in a cruddy mood all day. I was hoping painting would cheer me up. But so far, all I've done is paint a weeping willow that's truly crying because of how damn dark the picture is. A frown mars my face as I realize there's no fixing this.

I don't know what's wrong with me.

"Pulsators, huh?" I ask halfheartedly. "That's a new one." I shake my head as I set my brush down into the cup, dismayed with my lack of progress.

I pull my hair over my shoulder and twirl the ends as she continues, "Yeah. It's a little ball that goes into your cooch and vibrates." I stare at Natalie, slowly processing what she's saying. Thank fuck I have her as my roommate, sharing a two-bedroom apartment together in the middle of downtown. We split the rent to make costs bearable. But more than that, she's been my friend for years, even through the darker times when I pushed her away. We picked up everything right where we left off when we reconnected.

Right now, I just don't give a shit about whatever sex toy party she went to last night.

I clear my throat, trying to muster an ounce of her excitement as I say, "That sounds . . . fun."

Natalie pouts, her eyes dimming with concern. "What's wrong, Ari? Considering the stuff you're into," she says, eyeing me curiously, "I thought something like that would be right up your alley."

I feel like shit, but I just want to be alone. "I feel off. I'm just tired." I swirl the brush in the dirty cup to get some of the paint off the bristles. I speak without looking up, staring at the murky water. "I think I need some sun or something." I didn't expect her to come in here and join me, but I wasn't going to tell her no. Natalie's frown deepens and then she looks past me toward my bedroom door. "I'm sorry I'm being such a downer, Nat," I say, flashing her a weak smile. "I just feel like I woke up on the wrong side of the bed or something."

Nat stares at me for a long moment, chewing on the inside of her cheek before finally saying, "I'm a little worried about you, Ari." Her voice is delicate and cautious, but she doesn't need to be. I'm okay. I'm not where I was before.

I wave off her concern. "Don't be. I'm good." I nod at my canvas. "Just let me finish this up." I stare at the painting for a minute before pursing my lips. I should probably just trash it or paint the whole damn thing white and start over.

Nat gazes at me with suspicion. "You sure?"

I nod, picking my paintbrush back up and pressing the bristles against the side of the cup to get rid of most of the water. "Yeah. Tell me more about the party," I say, trying to change the subject back to her preference—sex. "It sounds like it was a lot of fun."

Nat nods, but her enthusiasm from earlier is dimmed, which makes me feel like shit. I hate spreading negativity.

I avoid her gaze entirely, shoving up my sleeves to add a bit of white paint to the background of the canvas. "It was. There's a bonus right now—" Nat pauses and reaches out for my arm, her fingers wrapping just below my elbow. Her grip is so strong she nearly pulls me backward. "What the hell happened to your arm?" Although it's a question, there's an accusation underlying her words as she stares at my arm in horror.

Shit. I pull away from her grasp, clenching my teeth and feeling a bit irritated. A bit ashamed. My heart is still lodged in my throat and I can't respond for a moment. I'm feeling her judgment.

I part my lips to reply, to make up some lie, some defense, but then close them. Nat's seen the bruises before. This is nothing new. She knows where they come from, and she knows that they're there with my consent. That it's just a kink.

I try to swallow, but my throat is dry. I hate how she does this to me. She makes me feel guilty.

Nat places her hands on her hips and glowers at me when I offer no response. "Well? And don't tell me it was just how you and Danny like to play," she says, but her voice cracks with pain. Her nostrils flare as she glares at my arm. "I don't believe it. Not this time." A part of me loves her for caring. Another part wants her to fuck off. We've gone around and around with this issue. It's how I've dealt with it all. It's the one thing that worked. Or used to work.

The very mention of his name sends a chill down my spine and causes my skin to prick with anxiety, although it never used to. If it weren't for Danny, I wouldn't be here. He helped me when I was at my lowest point in my life, saving me from darkness that was on the verge of swallowing me whole. There's no reason I should feel like this, but I do. I feel . . . afraid.

I pull my sleeve down, focusing on breathing and ignoring her. I need to talk to him. I'm not into this lifestyle like he is. It worked for a while, so he was right about giving it a shot. I'm just not sure I want to keep doing it.

But I owe him. And he's made it clear that he doesn't want to stop. Even if there's no sexual pleasure in it. He's not my boyfriend. Only my Master. He gives me the release I need to get rid of this sadness through an outlet of pain. But it's not working anymore. I don't know what changed.

"It's nothing," I say hastily, quick to cut her off the path she's heading down.

"Nothing?" Nat asks in disbelief. "That looked like a hell of a lot more than nothing."

I give her a big fake smile in an attempt to put her at ease, trying to hide the anxiety that's twisting my stomach. "It's not though. Trust me. Really, it's nothing," I lie as my throat closes and my chest feels hollow, "I enjoyed it, actually."

Natalie stares at me for a long time, her big brown eyes roving my face, searching for honesty.

Finally, she shakes her head, and the moment she does, I feel a wave of relief. I can't lose her. I have no one else. *No one but Danny*. Even though I don't want him anymore. Not like that though. I never wanted him *like that*. "I know this is supposed to be" —Nat takes in a breath as she looks to the door again and waves her hand in the air— "the thing you guys have, but I'll never be able to understand it. And quite frankly, it scares the shit out of me."

I don't blame her. Most people wouldn't understand. In fact, no one I know does. I don't even remember why I wanted this to begin with. He said it would heal me, and in a way, it did. But it's grown to be something different, and it doesn't feel like healing anymore. It's turned into something else. "But if it makes you happy and you're getting laid, I guess that's all that matters," Natalie mutters, clearly upset, but at least she's leaving it alone. I'm not getting laid, although she doesn't have to know the specifics. I'll fix this. I just need to tell Danny that I don't want it anymore and that I'm fine without it. Although I really don't know if I am fine. I will talk to him though . . . soon. I feel guilty for even thinking about it. Danny's done so much for me. I owe him my life. I feel ungrateful for wanting to complain, but it's time for me to move on.

"Maybe you should try it sometime," I suggest playfully, trying to lighten the tone, but I immediately regret it.

Natalie shakes her head vigorously. "Hell no. I like my vanilla sex with pulsators just fine, thank you very much. I'll leave that freaky shit to you." I huff out a dry chuckle, but I can't shake the feelings stirring in the pit of my stomach. I agreed to this M/s relationship. At times, I even wanted it. But now, I don't know how to get out.

"Ari?" Nat asks, breaking me out of my thoughts. I refocus my eyes on her face. "You sure you're okay,

Hun?" The words are on my lips. I could tell her everything about how I feel right now. Doing it would be like a weight lifted off my chest. I would finally have someone I could confide in about what's really going on in my life. But that's not what I do.

"Ari?" Nat presses when I don't respond. I flash her a smile and reply, "I'm fine." Deep down, I know I'm not.

CHAPTER 3

ZANDER

The Mercedes practically purrs as I park in the large, ten-story garage attached to the Parker business suite. This isn't the first time I've been in here. I don't own it, but I own plenty of men who sit behind the desks in this building.

And one of these fuckers is Danny Brooks.

The car door clicks shut and the alarm beeps as I walk across the concrete ground toward the entrance.

A smile creeps casually onto my lips as the greeter nods his head toward me, the automatic doors opening behind him. "Good evening, sir," he says in a raspy voice that's more comforting than anything else. His grey hair is barely noticeable under the tweed cap that matches his vest. As he smiles broadly at me, the wrinkles gather around his pale blue eyes.

"Good evening," I respond politely, heading straight into the building with a casual pep in my steps. The polished marble floors and stark white walls with gleaming steel-framed ceilings make the interior seem so much brighter. Every bit of light is reflected off every surface. The sounds of heels clicking, people chattering, and the large fountain in the center of the room spilling water over the edge immediately flood my senses.

It's almost five o'clock, close to quitting time, and for a Friday, the main lobby is fairly empty already. But I know Brooks is still here. Charles knows his routine. He's useful for that, and damn good at what he does.

I head straight to the far wall, my hands in my pockets and the hint of happiness on my face. Always smile. *Make them wonder what you're up to.* I remember the words my mother told me once. Back when I thought it was playful . . . when I thought she was happy. I didn't learn the darkness behind her words until much later. Until it was too late.

The elevator doors open and a man in a crisp grey suit exits, all the while loosening the black tie around his neck and holding his briefcase in his other hand. Two women exit behind him, walking closely and speaking in hushed voices. As I enter the empty carriage, I hear them laugh in unison, although it dims as the doors close, leaving me alone and in silence.

I push the button for the twenty-sixth floor, lighting up the ring around the number to bright green, and instantly, I'm ushered upward. My heart starts to race. It's not every day that I do this. In fact, it's a rarity. I hardly ever have to put pressure on my business associates, let alone make them fully aware that they can't fuck with me and my money.

I don't enjoy this aspect, but it's a necessity. If you let one man push you around, the others will know they can push you, too. And that can't happen. *Ever.*

It only takes one time to fall. One chance for them to knock you down and tear you apart. Like what happened with my mother. She let them see behind the cracks, and she never recovered.

I shove my hands back into my pockets. I'm still wearing thin leather gloves. It's not so uncommon for them to be worn this early in March. But inside the building, it's warm. And I don't need to be seen wearing them and drawing any suspicion.

Ding.

The twenty-sixth floor comes faster than I anticipated. Showtime.

My dress shoes slap on the hard slate floor as I walk past the two office spaces on my right. My shoulders are straight as I walk with ease past the large glass fronts of the offices. They're all nearly identical in appearance, neatly lined up rows of glass boxes. Each one houses some sort of profession. I stop abruptly and turn on my heels as I spot 2614.

Although my blood's heating, my heart's hammering, and I'm certain everyone can see the fire in my eyes, on the surface, I'm the same man I always am. Nonthreatening, happy. Not a care in the world.

I keep my hands in my pockets and rock on my heels as I smile down at the receptionist. Forcing the charm to stay in place.

"Mr. Payne," the young woman at the front of the office behind a small white desk greets as she rises to her feet, finally feeling my eyes on her. "May I take your coat?" she asks politely, already holding out her hand. I've been in here several times before, but this is the first time she's remembered who I am.

"No, thank you," I say easily. "I don't have an appointment. I was just hoping to catch Mr. Brooks before he left." I think the woman's name is Delores. I'm almost certain of it. My eyes flicker to the name on her desk plate and I see it there, in thick, bold letters. "I appreciate it though, Delores." She brightens at the use of her name. "Do you know if he's in?" I ask as I turn from her slightly, angling my body so she knows I'm headed that way.

"He is." She nods happily and takes a seat, scooting her chair back in.

"Have a wonderful weekend," I tell her, dipping my head and walking off as she calls out, "You too, Mr. Payne!"

My feet move of their own accord, everything seeming to narrow in my vision. The sound of my shoes against the thin, cheap carpet is being drowned out by the white noise ringing in my ears.

As soon as I stand in front of his door, every ounce of the facade is gone. I knock once, but I don't wait for a response. Instead, I open the door and walk in, kicking it shut behind me as I put my hands back into my pockets.

I casually look over at Danny Brooks, who at first seems shocked but then annoyed.

"I'm not sure if you could hear me, Mr. Payne." Brooks starts to speak while his eyes are on me, but then he looks back at his screen and begins typing, the sound of tiny clicks accompanying his voice, "But I'm currently busy."

"I got your message," I tell him with my hands still hidden.

Brooks barely looks up to acknowledge me, his head still down as he types on the computer without pausing to answer me. "You'll have to make an appointment," he says, and his voice is low as he blows me off. It's easy for associates to do when they first meet me and before they've finished doing business with me.

I walk slowly to the side of his desk, and it's only then that he stops, his fingers hovering just above the keys. His lower back presses into the thin leather seat, making it creak as he sits straighter and finally acknowledges me. "Yes, it's going to take a little longer than I anticipated." He pinches the bridge of his nose as if I'm a bother to him. As if my mere presence has caused him undue distress or a headache.

The smile finally grows on my face as he continues to underestimate me.

"You aren't able to make the payment?" I ask him, although it's a question, not a statement. My feet move slowly, taking steady strides, rounding his desk but still staying a few feet away, seemingly nonthreatening as I casually lean back against the wall.

"I don't believe so." He types a word, maybe two, and then gives me a look of irritation as he turns in his seat and lets out an exasperated sigh. "What can I do for you, Mr. Payne?" he asks in a voice laced with condescension.

I love it, the irony of it. But that's how men like him behave. They act as if *they* own you. When really, they don't have a damn thing to their name, and *you* own them.

I shrug and look to my left. The blinds to his small window are closed, so the office is rather dark and quiet. It's nearly perfect. But the walls are thin. Luckily, it's past five on a Friday and Mr. Brooks is surrounded by empty office spaces.

I walk closer to him as I speak with an even cadence. "Why is the payment delayed?" I ask him, as if I'm curious. As if it's acceptable to go back on our deal. As if it's fine to piss away half a million that he can't afford to pay back.

The fucker scoffs at me and rolls his eyes.

I don't hesitate to rip my hand from my pocket, grab the back of his head, and slam it on the desk. Once, then again. There's no blood. His nose didn't even hit the hard wood surface, only his forehead.

He's merely dizzy as I grab him by the collar and pull him up so his face is just beneath mine. "Was it a sure bet?" I ask him, my voice a sneer. My muscles are tight and coiled. I'm on edge and seeing nothing but red now.

"Zander—" he begins, and my name is a strained plea.

Brooks starts to speak, but I don't give him a moment to continue. I push him backward, his chair rolling across the floor as the backs of his knees smack against it. "There are no *sure bets*." I push the words through clenched teeth.

It wouldn't have come to this if he'd at least shown respect. It wasn't his money to piss away.

My grip tightens as I haul his back against the wall, slamming his spine against the drywall and denting it from the force. My teeth clench as my left hand forms a fist and I land a blow into his kidney. My muscles are taut and adrenaline is rushing through me. My head feels light. My breathing is heavy.

A loud grunt spills from his lips until I tighten my hand around his throat, feeling his blood rushing just beneath the surface and his throat giving in to the brute force of my weight. Both of his hands instantly reach for my hand on his neck, his blunt fingernails scratching against the glove on my hand. It's no use. I'm not letting go until he receives this message loud and clear.

I lean in close to his ear and hiss between clenched teeth, "You'll pay me all of it by the twenty-fifth of April. Or I'll destroy you." I pull away to look into his eyes. The milky whites have turned red around the edges, his face is a brighter shade of red, and his hands are still struggling at my grip. I hold his eyes, so full of sheer terror, only for a moment longer before releasing him.

I leave him there, heaving for air in a slump on the floor as I walk quickly to the door, shaking out my hand and ignoring the force inside me begging to unleash itself. Begging for a fight.

"Wait. I have something you may want," Brooks calls out in a croak. His words stop me midstep, but I continue momentarily, ignoring him and turning the doorknob.

"I want my money, Brooks. I won't take anything else," I tell him firmly.

His eyes stare back at me with a darkness as I stand in the doorway.

"I know what you like most at the club," he says then noticeably swallows, the soft, sick sound filling my ears as he rights himself, still slumping against the wall.

"The club?" I ask flatly, my face devoid of emotion or interest.

"Club X," he says loudly and clearly. The name makes my blood run cold. I only go there to watch my investments, for appearances only. I'm not interested in anything beyond that, and I haven't taken part in any of the . . . activities for a reason.

"I know you like the Slaves." My eyes narrow, and I have to keep my feet planted before I crush this fucker's windpipe. Brooks continues, "But there aren't many. Take mine . . . for a month."

My heart beats loud in my chest and blood rushes in my ears as I finally move slightly backward onto my heels and open the door wider so I can leave this prick and get on with my life.

"You have until the twenty-fifth," I reiterate and turn my back to him.

"You don't want her then?" he asks with slight disbelief, and I quickly turn to face him when I hear him take a single step toward me. The moment my eyes lock with his, he freezes.

"No," I tell him with a chill in my voice. "You'll pay me what you owe me—"

"She'll go up for auction then." He nods sternly, not backing down from my cold gaze. "I'll get that money to you on time. I have three hundred thousand coming. She's good for the rest. I know she is."

His admission makes rage and adrenaline pump through my blood. "That's not *your* money," I answer him.

He shrugs slightly, seemingly more at ease now that he's figured out a way to pay me. "She's mine. She'll do what she's told."

"On the twenty-fifth, Brooks," I say one last time, turning and closing the door behind me as I go.

I'm on edge and uneasy as I slip the gloves off and shove them into my pockets. My strides are larger than normal, the outrage apparent no matter how much I'd like to hide it. As I pass the rows of desks, I know they can see me. The real me, but in this moment, I can't suppress it. I can only move faster and leave before I turn around and do something I'll truly regret.

CHAPTER 4

ARIANNA

Whack!

A strangled cry escapes my lips as my head falls backward, the stinging pain racing up my ass cheeks, spreading out to my lower back and traveling downward through my thighs. *Fuck*. It hurts.

My breath comes out in short gasps as I try to bear the wave of stinging aftershocks, my face twisted into a tight mask of pain. I try to remember to give my worries to Danny. To relax and trust him that the pain will give me pleasure in the end. It's all for a reason. Everything happens for a reason and I deserve this, but in the end, it'll be all right.

That's what I used to tell myself, and it did bring me relief in the past. At times, I even looked forward to it. I deserved this, and the result lifted a weight from me. It was freeing. But not now. It's only mind-numbing agony now.

My heart skips a beat as I sense movement. And I brace for another one. But it doesn't come right away.

I can hear Danny behind me, his breathing deep and ragged, stalking me like I'm a wild animal that needs to be put down. But he doesn't have to do that. I'm chained to the wall, my hands cuffed above my head, my bare ass behind me, giving him complete access. He just likes doing this. He likes building the anticipation of a hit, but never striking until I least expect it.

I hate it. As I wait for his next blow, I can't remember what I used to think about during these times. I don't remember them. *It wasn't like this.*

I wait in agony, my limbs taut and sweaty, knowing the next one is coming, even if I don't know when. I hear his footsteps move to my right side and then to my left. Then I sense him directly behind me. The sound of his breathing fills my ears and my heart pounds faster. It's coming. Everything goes silent.

A drop of sweat runs down my forehead, down my nose, all the way down my chin, and drops to the plush carpet below. I swear my heart is about to race out of my chest as I wait, thumping so loudly that I know he hears it. I feel dizzy as I grip the chains, bracing myself for what's to come.

"You're holding back," his voice calls out from behind me. My body relaxes at his words. *I am.* He knows me so well. "You need to give in," he tells me.

My head hangs in shame. This is my fault. I used to be ready for this, willing to give him my pain, and it would make me feel better.

An animalistic grunt splits the air, followed by multiple lashes.

A tortured scream tears from my throat. Agony becomes my existence, my ass, thighs, and lower back radiating a pain so strong my knees buckle. The hard cast iron cuffs scrape my skin as the full weight of my body pulls down toward the floor, my hands stretching out above my head as far as they'll go.

I try to silence my pain as the unforgiving metal digs into my skin. Danny's behind me, his breathing heavier and more shallow than before. I know he's getting off on this. His cock is hard as a fucking rock. It was the trade-off. He'd take the pain of my past away in exchange for this.

The words are on my lips. I need to tell him, to let him know that I'm not okay and I can't give in like I used to. I don't want this anymore. *But what about everything he's done for you?* that annoying voice at the back of my head chimes in. *You wouldn't be here if not for him. And he knows what you need. You're only in this position because you won't listen.*

"Listen to me," Danny says softly, almost in a comforting voice as he cradles my chin in his hand. As if he knew exactly what I was thinking just now. "Give in to the pain, and it will set you free."

A feeling of guilt presses down upon my chest and I suck in a ragged breath. I hate it. I hate it even more because I know it's true. I wouldn't be here if Danny hadn't saved me. For a time, he made me forget the terrible loss I suffered. He made me feel like I'd repented in a way.

The sound of Danny moving again breaks me out of my preoccupation. I almost shake my head and tell him I can't. No. Not again. I don't think I can take anymore. I stay half-slouched. I don't have the energy to stand up straight. I just can't.

"Raise your ass," I hear Danny's deep voice command behind me. Goosebumps rise on my thighs as I tremble at the anger lacing his words. I want to tell him no. I want to tell him that I can't do this anymore. But the words stick in my throat when I try to speak them. He has my best intentions at heart. He did in the beginning, and this must be my fault. I'm the one holding back. I'm not well, and he knows it.

I try to rise and straighten my body, my legs wobbling like Jell-O. It's a chore to arch my back. I manage, but it's all I can do to keep myself in position. I weakly grip the chains that are holding me up, my limbs completely covered in sweat, my heart racing so fast that the room spins around me. *He saved me. He saved me. He saved me*, I chant over and over in my mind, mentally preparing myself for this. But the blow never comes. Suddenly, I'm being released from the chains, Danny appearing at my side and jerking my cuffs loose. I gasp as he gently lowers me to the floor, hitting the plush carpet with a thud. My hands immediately go to my wrists. There are deep red indentations from when I strained against them, but they're not as bad as I thought. They still hurt like hell though. I look up, taking in my surroundings, my breathing ragged. We're in one of Club X's private rooms, one of Danny's favorites. It's absolute luxury, with a king-size bed in the middle of the room adorned with grey and white silk bedding and ultra-plush pillows.

A large canopy frames the sides with gossamer white curtains tied back against each post.

The walls match the colors of the bedding, grey and white, and have intricate designs, adding that much more luxury in the fine details. The floor is covered with thick, soft white carpet and the matching furniture is chic and contemporary, with a large loveseat at the foot of the bed and an oversized chair near the granite fireplace.

Then there are the toys.

A delicate glass china cabinet sits on the left side of the room, filled with whips, riding crops, and other devices. Nearby, there is a grey rack with white shackles.

And above me is the Saint Andrew's Cross that chained me to the wall. Plus, Danny.

His gaze holds nothing but disappointment. I look back at him, unable to control the anxiety I feel along with the pain. Although I'm naked, bared before him, he's dressed in grey dress pants and a white dress shirt that's unbuttoned at the chest, his dark blond hair adorned by his cold, piercing hazel eyes. "What's wrong?" I dare ask, my voice sounding like a small, scared child's. And I truly am scared. I don't know what to think anymore.

"You," he says simply. "You're not behaving. You're making this harder than it has to be."

"Sir, I—"

"I only want to help you. I know you need this. You aren't well, Arianna."

"I–I—," I protest, trying to put some strength in my words but failing. He's right. I'm not okay, but I just don't know if this is the answer.

"You don't trust me as a Master. I've done so much for you." I feel tears form in my eyes at his words.

"Danny, please, it's not like that. It's just . . ."

Danny leans forward, putting his face close to mine. The hurt in his expression is nothing compared to the anger in his blazing eyes. "It's just what?" he asks.

Tell him. He needs to know.

A lump forms in my throat, but I manage to mumble, "I feel like this isn't working anymore, and it hurts, but there's no . . . there's nothing but pain. I didn't tell you because I don't want to upset you."

"It's only because you aren't trusting me." His voice is full of conviction. "Don't you remember how freeing it is? Why are you hurting yourself?"

After a moment, he takes a step back and stands up straight. "This has been coming for a long time now." His words are terrible. Not because they're angry, but because they're so quiet and fill me with overwhelming anxiety.

"What do you mean—"

Danny walks forward and unbuckles the thick leather collar from around my neck.

"Danny, what are you doing?" I cry in panic. I reach up to try to stop him, but he swats my hand away as easily as one would swat a fly and pulls the collar free from my neck, leaving cold air to replace its warmth. He steps back with it clenched tightly in his hand, scowling at me with a coldness I've never seen from him before. Unconsciously, my hands fly to my neck. It feels so strange, running my fingers along the bare skin there. It feels . . . empty. Like he's abandoning me.

"I told you so long as you didn't give up on yourself, I wouldn't give up on you." His words are carried with pain. He's given up on me.

My heart feels like it's been pierced by a jagged spear.

His next words turn my blood to ice. "You're going up for auction."

My jaw goes slack as what he says registers, my heart skipping several beats as I'm shocked into silence.

"You need to learn to trust me," Danny says. "And I think handing you over to another Master is the best thing for you right now."

I stare at him in disbelief, hardly believing what he's saying.

"I want you to know what it's like to miss me," he says. "To realize how good you had it."

But it's been so bad, I want to tell him, *so bad that I want to leave you.*

For weeks, I've thought about ending this, but the fear of losing him and having no one who truly knows me kept me from doing it. To me, being with someone who doesn't know my history is terrifying.

"You can come back to me after you've learned your

lesson," Danny says. "Maybe then you'll truly appreciate me."

"Danny—" I try to say.

He waves me silent. "I'm done. Prepare yourself for your auction."

With that said, he walks out, closing the door behind him.

I sit there on the floor, my skin prickling as a torrent of emotions goes through me. Anxiety. Anger. Sadness.

I don't know what to do. I'm so used to leaning on Danny for support to conquer my demons that I don't know if I can survive without him.

CHAPTER 5

ZANDER

The chill of the wind whips across my face, the hairs on the back of my neck standing to attention. The thick wool overcoat I have on shields everything but my neck and cheeks. I don't move to cover them though. The crisp morning air seems fitting as I stare down at my mother's gravesite. I was only ten when she died. I wonder what kind of man I'd be if she'd never left.

My heart beats slower as another gust of wind comes, harsher this time. Again, I don't move. I stand still, my hands shoved into my coat pockets.

I have her tombstone memorized, but my eyes still flicker over the engraved message.

Marie Payne

1958 - 1994

Loving wife, doting mother.

She will be missed.

I do miss her, as odd as it may be. I hardly knew her, but I miss what could have been. She's the one who taught me to smile behind the pain. She never stopped until the last few weeks of her life. It all crumbled around her, the affair that tore them apart. People were always watching. Always judging. It was too much for her.

I clear my throat as I straighten my stance and take in a deep breath. When I come here, the smile that's perpetually on my face is nowhere to be found. I can't do it. I can't bring myself to smile when I'm around her.

Maybe that's why I come here so much.

I don't know much about her, if I'm honest with myself. There's plenty online, so I suppose I know as much about her as a stranger would who wanted to look her up. She had no family but us. She married into wealth and gave the Payne heir a baby boy. And then she had miscarriage after miscarriage.

Her name means misery. *Marie.* I remember she told me that once, and I didn't understand what she meant at the time. It's the Latin meaning. The sadness in her pale eyes is something that haunts me even till this day. How could my father not see it?

He'll never admit it, but I know she killed herself. He wouldn't let her leave. I remember the fights, the screams. That's what I remember most, even if I always had my eyes closed tight and my small hands over my ears. I'll never forget the way they'd raise their voices until I knew it must have hurt them.

I'd hide in the closet of my room whenever it happened.

I stare at the small crack in the marble slab of her tombstone.

I never understood why they hated each other so much. Why they enjoyed hurting each other with their words. They must've—fighting was all they ever did.

My eyes settle onto the line that reads, *doting mother*.

I think children have to love their mother. It's something in them that's biological. It must be so, because I know I love her. Even without a single memory of her gentle touch or soothing words. I haven't a single one. The nannies were there for me when I was young. But they came and went like a merry-go-round. They got *too attached*.

The only constant was the fighting between my parents, and when that came to a halt with her death, there was only silence for a short time. And then my father started with me.

"*One mistake and you're ruined*," he'd tell me all the time. I was to be perfect. Just like my mother was supposed to be.

I was good where my mother failed. I enjoyed charming people. I liked getting a reaction from them. I liked for them to see the boy I wanted to be, and not the hollow shell I became.

It's less amusing now, but it's vital to my survival.

Father taught me well.

My phone pings with a message at the thought, and I'm

slow to pull it out, even though my fingers are already wrapped around it.

When I finally take my eyes from the tombstone to look at it, a text from my father stares back at me.

Dinner on the 7th for the gala. You need to be there.

A grunt leaves me and I roll my eyes as I ignore it. I already know about the event. I'll be there just like I always am.

"He's still the same," I tell my mother as if she can hear me. I don't even remember why I came today. Some days just take me here. Usually when I'm not paying attention, or looking for a moment to think.

My father needs me now more than ever. As he grows old and his influence is waning, he's relying on me to a greater extent. I don't mind it. In my mind, I've always needed to step up. *If only I had back then.*

But this constant bitching and reminding me is unnecessary. I swipe away the text.

I nearly shove my phone back into my coat pocket, ready to shield my bare hands from the wind, but the picture of *her* is on my screen. *Arianna Owens.*

And with those gorgeous eyes staring back at me, I'm reminded of the last thing I care to remember. My mistake. Danny Brooks. I stare at my phone in my hand, the dim glow lighting the darkened sky. Isaac looked her up and gave me her information. *Arianna Owens.* I suppose in a way, she reminds me of my mother. There's a sadness there. Something that haunts her. She makes me feel like she needs to be saved.

I pinch the bridge of my nose, feeling ridiculous. "This is your fault," I say out loud, my voice drowned out by the harsh gusts of the wind.

She's beautiful, but her gorgeous eyes are haunted by something, darkened by what lies behind them.

I'm still enraged that Brooks offered me a month with her in exchange for a debt of hundreds of thousands that he owes me. The only claim he has to her is the collar around her neck.

My dick hardens at the thought of her on her knees, giving herself to me, pleasing me. I've been tempted before at the club, though I've never taken part. At least not in the open like that. These men are foolish to show their cards. My good friend Lucian paid the price years ago. Although now it's paid off for him, the burden of his past only goes to show that NDAs are nothing more than paperwork. They have no loyalty to them, merely sheets of paper—so easily shredded, so quickly forgotten.

Arianna's haunted eyes shine through the screen, staring back at me. I've seen her before. I've watched the way he drags her through the halls and leads her to the dungeon. She's submissive in her nature, but I don't trust her or his offer. I don't let anyone close for a reason.

And women make men fall.

I pull the jacket tighter around me and shove the phone back into my pocket.

I should stay away. I should take the money and let him

fall on his own, carrying on with my life and ignoring the pathetic waste of life that is Danny Brooks.

But those eyes call to me. My contempt for him and what he represents make a side of me I try to keep suppressed rise to the surface.

And that's a very dangerous thing.

CHAPTER 6

ARIANNA

You're going up for auction.

Danny's words run through my mind as I scrub at the spaghetti-stained plate vigorously, my eyes unfocused as I stare straight ahead into the wall, the rough Brillo pad digging into my soft skin. I've been at this for hours now, cleaning piles of dirty dishes after a day of hard work at the local shelter.

It was a packed house today, causing more chores to be done at closing. This job pays shit, but I don't mind. I couldn't care less about the money. It's about giving back and making my life have meaning. Coming here has always been my therapy, a way to escape my emotions. It's been cathartic for me to help people who are down on their luck, and it eases some of the guilt that plagues me.

But not today.

I scrub the plate harder, a mix of pain and anger

running through my body. The whip marks are a mess of bruises along my back and thighs, and each small movement is accompanied with a hint of pain. It's a reminder that I'm alive, that I can *feel*.

I haven't been able to get my mind off Danny for more than a minute.

Even now, I can't believe what he said to me. That he's willing to put me up for auction like I'm just a commodity that can be bartered or sold at whim. And after everything we've been through. After everything he's done for me. All because I've been unhappy with our sessions. But I am broken. Something's changed, and I know I'm unhappy. What used to work isn't helping me anymore.

I suck in a painful breath as I look down at the plate that I'm scrubbing. The red stains are clinging stubbornly to the surface. No matter how hard I try, I can't seem to get them out. Just like how dark memories cling to me, sticking in my mind no matter how hard I try to rid myself of them.

If I could just forget. I drop the plate into the suds and let it fall to the bottom of the basin. My fingertips are pruned as I stare at them, remembering everything.

The thought summons a dark specter, one that always seems to pounce whenever I'm depressed.

I always had a drink in my hand. Even as I stumbled in my heels, a drink was sure to be there. Drugs? Yep. I was down for anything. I just wanted to fit in. I wanted others to accept me. I didn't go to college. I couldn't afford it, and it damn sure wasn't something my parents cared about. But I was at every party on campus.

That's where I met Natalie, although she just talked to me, bringing me into her group. It was different when she was there. It was better, but back then I didn't know. I just wanted to feel something. I needed something in my pathetic life.

I struggle against his powerful grip, my arms held back above my head against the bedpost, my eyes glazed and unfocused. I shouldn't be here alone in this darkened room with him, but I drank too much and let him talk me into it. Now I'm regretting it big time, but the words are lost in the haze of alcohol.

Chase lowers his handsome face down close to mine as the walls shake from the bass of the music blasting through the frat house. "God, I've wanted you all night," he says, kissing my neck, his breath hot against my skin. "You asked for this."

I shake my head weakly, insecurity twisting my stomach. I didn't want this. I'm not like that. I don't want to be thought of like that. I didn't know when he led me up here. How did I not know? My head shakes and I feel so stupid, so foolish. So guilty.

I part my lips to tell him, the alcohol making my head feel so heavy. But he kisses me instead and then pulls back to take his shirt off. No, I just need to tell him no. He'll listen. He's not trying to take advantage of me. It's my fault. "I thought you just wanted to mess around a little." My words come out muffled.

"What, baby?" he asks as he pushes my legs apart wider. I try to pull them closed, but his hips butt against mine. I was just looking to have a little fun.

His hands shove my skirt up and my arms are too heavy to push him away.

I didn't mean for it to go this far. I was reckless. It was my fault. I don't know if he heard me whispering no. It makes me feel a little better to think he didn't, and I don't know if that's more fucked up than the alternative.

My breathing is ragged as I shove the memory out of my mind and let go of the Brillo pad. There are red marks on my palm from where the pad has dug into my soft flesh, but I hardly notice it, a chill snaking down my spine. I stopped going to parties, but the reliance on drugs and alcohol didn't end. And one mistake led to another that I'll never forgive myself for. Even now, I still ache in my lower abdomen at the memory of waking up on a bloody mattress months later, my nightgown soaked with dark red blood. I didn't know I'd been pregnant until I had miscarried. More mistakes. More blame. More guilt.

That was enough to send me spiraling down into darkness. I just wanted to end it all. I had a bottle in my hand as my legs hung over the bridge. I'd drink the pain away and fall in. I was so done with making mistakes. But Danny saw me. *He saved me.*

And now . . . he's discarding me like none of that meant anything.

"Are you okay, dear?" a familiar voice asks, breaking me out of my dark trance. I whip my head around to see Clara, the head cook of the shelter, staring at me with concern. She's a large woman in her early fifties, with greying hair that's always arranged up high on her head in a loose bun. Her outfit, an oversized blue dress with a white apron, only makes her appear more matronly. She has a large oval-shaped face lined with gentle wrinkles, and her hair contains striking streaks of grey that give her a distinguished look. I flash her a modest smile I hope she thinks is real. I try my best to keep my troubles hidden whenever I'm here, or anywhere, really. I don't like to spread negativity. *Give your pain to me. Only me.* Danny's words from the night he first showed me the cane come back to me. I turn my back to her and grab the dish towel, drying my hands before turning back to face her. "I'm fine. Why, what's up?"

Clara nods at the dishes. "You seemed a bit distracted. You sure you're all right?"

I huff out a humorless chuckle. "Oh no, I just zoned out."

Clara places her hands on her wide hips, giving me a knowing look. "Are you sure you're okay?"

I flash her another smile, this one easier. "I'm positive."

For a moment, Clara looks uncertain as if she wants to press the issue, but then says, "Okay, I'm here for you if you ever need someone to talk to, okay, honey?"

Warmth spreads through my chest and it's hard not to let the emotions I'm feeling play across my face. It touches me that Clara cares at all about what I might be going through. But then again, she wouldn't be working at a pantry that fed the homeless if she didn't possess so much empathy. There are so many people here who need help. And not because they were careless and reckless and hurting the people around them. They didn't choose it.

"Okay," I tell her with gratitude, "I'll keep that in mind."

"Make sure that you do." Clara gives me a heartfelt smile before returning to her chores.

I spend the next half hour finishing cleaning up the last of the dishes and then head out behind the building with a bag of trash in my hand. It's full to the brim and heavy. I have to lift it with all of my weight to make sure it doesn't drag on the asphalt and tear open.

I step out into the back alley, my skin pricking from the cool air sweeping through the area, goosebumps rising on my flesh. A ray of moonlight shines down through the crack between the buildings, illuminating the walkway. I need to clean up back here. Pieces of newspaper and some rotten food are strewn about, and the smell from the nearby dumpsters assaults my nose as I make my way down the small steps onto the cold concrete path. My car is parked around the side of the building, and it's just a short walk through the alley to reach it. But I need to dump the trash bag first.

I'm in the process of closing it when suddenly, rough and firm hands grab me from behind, clamping down on my mouth to stifle my cry.

My heart pounds as panic overtakes me, and I struggle against my captor, but whoever it is is too strong. Subduing my attempts to escape, I hear a grunt as I'm picked up off my feet and pressed up against the stone wall, feeling a rock-hard body press into me from behind.

"Be a good girl," a familiar voice growls into my ear.

"Danny," I gasp with surprise, my heart hammering wildly as a hundred different dreadful thoughts run through my mind. I don't understand what's going on. "What are you doing here?" I cry.

Danny doesn't immediately respond, keeping me pressed up against the wall for several more moments, his breath hot on my neck. All the while, fear runs through me. He's never done anything like this before, and I can smell whiskey on his breath. He's taking joy out of keeping me guessing on his intentions while increasing the pressure on my back.

"Danny, please," I whimper as the pain grows, my eyes darting to the back entrance of the shelter. "Sir, please." I don't know what's going on. This isn't him.

Finally, he lets me go.

I gasp as I come free, turning around to face him, my chest heaving from my ragged breaths.

Danny's scowling at me, his hazel eyes blazing with anger. He looks out of place in this trashy alley with his expensive dress pants and shirt, his hair slicked to the side. I can even smell his vintage cologne over the filthy aroma of garbage.

"I've come to remind you how ungrateful you are," he growls. His words sting with a pain so raw, I can hardly stand up straight.

"Danny—" I pause and swallow the lump growing in my throat. I'm grateful. I am. I truly am.

"Don't you remember?" he asks me, gesturing around the grimy alley. "This is the same fucking alleyway I found you in. Before you went to the bridge. You were poor, broke, hungry, and homeless. And I was the only one who was stupid enough to have pity for you."

I shake my head, unable to understand how differently Danny's treating me. He's never been this cruel and hateful with me before. "Danny, please. It's not like that." My eyes dart from him to the door. There's a single light shining above it, and everything in me is pleading with me to run. But it's Danny. He saved me. He won't hurt me. "Why are you so angry with—"

"Did you once try to call me since taking your collar?" he demands, cutting me off. "Did you once try to beg me to take you back?"

"But you said I was going up for auction—" I try to reason with him. I don't know what to do. I'm so lost.

"I fed you, you ungrateful bitch!" Danny snarls, spittle flying from his mouth. "Helped you when no one else would. And look at you, ready to run from me the first chance you get."

I gape at him with shock.

"I saved you!" He continues his rant. "You were nothing but a drunk degenerate when I found you. And if it weren't for me, you'd be fucking dead!" His words cut through me because they're true.

Tears burn my eyes as I gaze into his rage-filled face.

"Danny, please," I beg, a huge lump choking my throat as I reach my hands out to him imploringly. "Please calm down and just listen to me . . ."

"No," Danny fumes. "I'm sick of listening to your pathetic whining."

"But—"

Danny rushes forward, grabbing me by the neck, and slams me back up against the wall. A gasp escapes my lips as pain radiates up my back and I struggle to pry his powerful hands free of my throat.

"Shut. The. Fuck. Up," he says nastily in my face, the smell of whiskey hitting me even harder now, his eyes blazing with a hatred that tears at my heart. "Your voice is *so* fucking annoying. I can't believe I listened to that shit for nearly two years. It's like nails on a fucking chalkboard."

Tears start streaming down my face as I choke against his grasp. His words are so biting and cruel.

"I just want to remind you that even though you're going up for auction, I still fucking own you," he barks. "I don't give a fuck whose collar you have around your neck. You're fucking mine. You got it?"

I'm unable to respond, his grip on my neck so strong that I can barely breathe.

He pulls me forward and then slams me back against the wall with enough force that it jars my teeth.

"I said you got it?" he repeats with fury. "The money is

mine, and so are you. This is a fucking lesson and nothing else. I own you!"

"Yes," I croak, my eyes stinging and my lungs refusing to fill.

Danny holds me there for a moment, applying more and more pressure to my throat until I think I'm going to pass out. He lets me go at the last possible second, and I fall away from the wall, sinking to my knees onto the grungy ground, gasping, choking, and crying.

"You'll do well to remember that," Danny tells me, uncaring that I'm bawling my eyes out at his feet, "because if you don't, you're going to wish I left you for dead."

"You're going up for auction, and then you're coming back to me."

I nod my head vigorously, needing him to know I'm obeying. I'm listening. "Yes, Sir." I croak out the words through the pain.

"There, there." His voice softens. "I don't know why you do this to yourself. All you have to do is listen." I hear his words, so gentle and comforting. *Just listen*. But everything in me is telling me to run. This isn't right.

"I'm sorry I'm so hard on you. I just know you aren't well." He crouches beside me and I flinch as he grips my chin in his hand. "You need me, you need this."

I nod my head as much as I can, staring into his eyes. But I see through him. In a split second, I see through it all. It's about the money. It hits me so hard, so brutally, that I can't hide my expression.

His face morphs from the gentle attitude to one of cruelty. "You're going up there, Arianna." His voice is low. "I know where you live. I saved your life. It belongs to me now."

A feeling of despair washes over me as I choke on my tears, my neck throbbing.

"Just do what I say and everything will be all right."

CHAPTER 7

ZANDER

My hand has been forced in some ways. Well, not quite. I pick up the beer bottle and bring it to my lips as I sit at the table in the far-right corner of the upper floor in Club X. *The auction room.*

I've never felt as if my hand's been forced. There's always a choice. However, it's undeniable that I'm backed in a corner with the knowledge that Arianna Owens will be on the stage soon. Sold to the highest bidder, and if it's anyone else, that will be the money I'm paid.

"What are you going to do?" Charles asks. He's seated next to me at the small circular table. There are dozens of tables in the room that seat only two to three men at most. A mask covers his face just like most of the men here, including me. They all know who I am, but with his face completely covered by the smooth, flat black mask that hides every inch of his features with the exception of his mouth, they have no idea who I'm seated with. He's lucky in that respect.

My fingers trail along my jaw, the hint of stubble rough beneath my fingertips. "I haven't decided," I answer him honestly.

He grunts a laugh and sits back in his seat, picking up the pamphlet to the auction and skimming the lines. I've done the same so many times when I didn't give a fuck about sitting here. Just doing my part to fit in and keeping my friends company while I take notes about the perversions of the other men in the room. *Always watching.*

I've never shown my cards. I've never given them an ounce of useful information to use against me if they so choose.

"I can't believe a place like this exists," Charles mutters under his breath. I turn to him, ignoring Madam Lynn, the owner of Club X, as she starts the show. I've seen these auctions a million times. I've never given a fuck about them. It's mostly a charade, no surprise at all who will end up with whom.

My shoulders rise in a shrug. It's a fantasy really. Decorated and maintained to provide a false sense of a world that's temporary. Darkened rooms for men to spend their money and sate themselves, safety for women who want to give in to their dark desires. It's all an illusion, nothing more than that.

But as the first woman is sold as the hammer is dropped, I find my heart beating faster. The auction has never felt more real than in this moment.

The men are talking quietly to themselves. Arianna is next, according to the pamphlet. None of their eyes are on me. Instead they're focused on Brooks, who's seated on the far side of the room, at the table farthest away from me. His foot is tapping nervously on the floor as he leans back in his seat with a cigar, putting on a casual air. As if his very life doesn't depend on Arianna being sold to pay his debt.

I imagine most of the men here expect him to bid on her. Like it's a game between them. It wouldn't be the first time a Dominant or Master has sent his partner to the auction, some for play, others for punishment. But when he doesn't bid on her, the mood in the room will change. Each second that passes, taking me closer and closer to that moment, heightens my anxiety.

I can already feel the tense air growing as the men each decide for themselves if they're willing to take her.

She's the epitome of what a submissive should be. Or slave, rather. Since that's the preference she's taken at the club. She's only ever been with him, but he's put on quite a show with her before.

"How many have you come to?" Charles asks me, his voice low. So low that the clinking of the ice in his short glass of bourbon nearly drowns out his words as he brings the glass to his lips.

Again, I shrug, lifting my beer bottle to my lips and taking a sip. I answer him with a low voice, "Too many."

"How many have you won?" he asks.

"None," I answer him with clarity, setting my glass on the white tablecloth and looking straight ahead. The thick red curtains are pulled back and the lights focused on the stage, just how it always is.

Charles laughs a deep, rough sound, and my eyes are pulled to his.

"How can you resist?" he asks with a warmth in his voice I've never heard before.

"Easy," I answer and take a quick look around the darkened room. "They're all watching."

"Let them see. Isn't that what this place is for?" He swirls the ice in his glass and drains the remainder of the bourbon as a waitress passes us. I eye him as he leans in her direction, ordering another. He seems more comfortable behind the mask than I've ever seen him before. As if it grants him a freedom he's never had. And I suppose it does. For him and many of the other men in here.

But I know all of the men in this room, and I'm not foolish enough to think that an NDA is enough to keep loose lips from using information within the walls of Club X as blackmail. As much as I'm fond of Madam Lynn, many things are beyond her control.

The first woman is sold to her own Dominant and the second is a new girl, unclaimed and looking a bit shy. She goes for a higher sum, having multiple bidders as the waitress comes back with another drink for Charles. No surprise there, and nothing out of place. Madam Lynn's expression reflects exactly what I'm feeling as Arianna walks out onto the stage.

The lights are focused on her, making her sun-kissed

skin seem to glow. She takes in a shaky breath as she stands there, and her ankles cross and uncross as she clasps her hands in front of her. Everything slows down as her thin black dress swirls along her upper thighs. With the lights so bright, her vision is limited. It will take her a moment to adjust to the darkness in the crowd beyond the stage. But she's not trying. *She doesn't want to see.*

"We'll start the bidding at fifty thousand dollars," the auctioneer says.

Madam Lynn's gaze is focused on Brooks. She doesn't like surprises, and she's not used to them either. For a woman who's so submissive in nature, she controls every aspect of the club with an iron fist. But this is out of her control, and her resentment of that is reflected in her eyes.

The small room is quiet. A man clearing his throat and the skinny black heels shifting on the large stage ahead of us are the only sounds as the men wait to see what Brooks is up to. He takes a long and deep puff of his cigar, keeping his eyes on Arianna, who's looking straight ahead at the barren wall in front of her.

After a moment, he crosses his arms, ignoring the men and looking uninterested.

"Five hundred thousand." The auctioneer gestures to a man in the back. I take a quick look, not turning in my seat to see it's Nathan Blanchard. He's a simple man, vanilla in tastes, but he has no knowledge of what it means to be faithful.

"Six," a man across the room says as he raises his

paddle. I recognize his voice, as do most of the men here. That's the thing about masks. When the circles in the business world are so small, you can't hide behind a thin piece of plastic or leather.

A third man raises his paddle, and I take another drink. Listening to the auctioneer and glancing at Brooks, who's merely smiling, confident his prized possession will buy him out of the debt he's in.

Each bid feels like a slap to my face.

Whoever wins her will use her for his own enjoyment. However he'd like. Of course, there's a contract, set terms that Arianna will agree to. Her preferences are all laid out in the pamphlet sitting in front of me and in front of all the attendees. And she agreed to this. But I see the look in her eyes, and I know the way he treats her. *I know her past.* This isn't right.

I'm not interested in their money. My teeth grind against one another as the paddles continue to raise, the amount increasing with each bid.

The next two bids make my back straighten. My muscles are getting more and more tense.

Arianna's shoulders are rigid, but she stands tall, looking utterly gorgeous in the thin black chemise with a black rose held in front of her. Maybe it makes me a sick fuck, but the sadness only makes me want her more.

I raise my paddle, not uttering a word. It won't be the first time I've bid. But my normal cocky grin is absent. I'm not just fucking with someone as I usually am when I bid.

I've done that before, more than a few times, although I always know the man I'm screwing with. It's always been in jest and lighthearted. But the winning bidder looks over his shoulder at me with disdain, and it's hard to keep the emotions off my face.

"Don't lose your cool," I hear Charles say as he lifts the glass to his lips.

I lean back in my seat and force a smirk on my lips.

None of these men know what's going on. They can think I've finally decided to indulge, but then they'll have ammunition. They'll use it against me.

From the corner of my eye, another paddle is raised.

"One point ten," the auctioneer's voice sounds out. "One twenty." I hear his voice over the loud ringing in my ears. My eyes focus on Arianna's. My heart beats slower, louder, drowning out everything else as I watch her close her eyes.

She's not meant for this. This isn't right. There's such an innocence about her, a vulnerability. I want to save her. I really shouldn't, since winning her will taint my reputation. I need to play this right.

It's just a deal I made with a man I shouldn't have. An error on my part. How many more mistakes can I afford?

"Going once," the auctioneer yells out. The sight of Arianna's large doe eyes opening and shining with fear is what breaks me from my thoughts. The quiet of the room comes back to me. The faint sounds of men drinking and hushed conversations fill the darkened room once again.

I can't let her pay for my sins.

I raise my paddle, and the auctioneer points in my direction.

"One point three million."

"One point four." I hear Brooks's voice, and it pisses me off. I lower my paddle and notice the way the other three men who were bidding look at him. As if they're not sure they want to press on. As if it was just a game to them. A rather expensive one.

"One point five," the auctioneer says as one of the other bidders raises his paddle.

I don't hesitate. "One point six million dollars."

"You look pissed," Charles tells me, not so quietly. It's an effort to smirk and look over at Brooks with a smile on my face, as if I'm merely playing. As if all the world is a game to me. Playing the part of a spoiled rich boy without a care in the world.

If only they knew.

Brooks plays with his paddle as if debating upping the amount. He can. And I can choose not to bid again. I can let him hang himself, but then his poor Arianna will go back to him.

Why is she even with him?

"Going once."

I hadn't questioned her motives before, but as the thought hits me, she could be in on this. The corners of my lips nearly drop as the auctioneer calls out, "Going twice."

They could be playing me for a fool. And I've just given them exactly what they wanted.

My blood chills as the realization washes over me. And I played into their hands because of her. Because of the thought of someone else having her.

"Sold!"

And I let them play me. I've never felt so fucking stupid before . . . but now that she's mine, I'll have to play this right. It's all about appearances. That's all it's ever been about.

My reputation, my family name—it's all on the line.

I'm simply a rich boy who fell for a woman and couldn't resist her.

This can't come back as a perversion. I crack my knuckles, one at a time. The only way to get around that is to be seen with her. Constantly. And not in fucking Club X.

CHAPTER 8

ARIANNA

The scribble of a pen going across paper fills the room. *Scratch. Scratch. Scratch.* Anxiety twists my stomach as I watch Madam Lynn flip through the papers of my contract, signing where needed, her finely sculpted right brow arched in concentration. Her dark blonde hair is pulled into an elegant side ponytail and her makeup is dramatic yet flawless, her lips painted a bright shade of red. A diamond cocktail ring adorns her finger and a sparkling cuff that mimics a submissive's adorns her right wrist, while her strong, yet simple fragrance tickles the tip of my nose.

The creak of a chair breaks me out of my reverie and I freeze, my skin pricking. I feel fucking sick.

He's watching me. It's all he's been doing since he stepped in the room. Watching me and saying nothing.

I try my best to avoid his gaze, my cheeks turning red, and I readjust the hem of my dress to cover more of my legs. But his piercing blue eyes seem to draw mine to them. They're beyond gorgeous, but more than that, they're hiding secrets. *Dark secrets.*

Just like I am. Just listen to him. Do as he says. I'll figure a way out of this. I just don't know how.

The breath stills in my lungs as our eyes meet, heat flushing my throat. I've seen many handsome men here in passing, those who were bold enough to remove their masks while at play, but Zander takes the cake. His dark hair is perfectly groomed, his chiseled jawline immaculately shaved, his prominent cheekbones sharp enough to cut glass. He's dressed in a crisp dark suit, the white dress shirt underneath the jacket unbuttoned at the front. It goes without saying that he's a man of power and wealth, but he exudes much more than that. There's an aura of enigma around him, an atmosphere so strong that it causes my pulse to race and makes me weak in the knees. Zander stares back at me with an intensity that causes my palms to feel clammy, my body temperature rising. Even while looking intense, he looks so calm and composed, his legs spread out wide as if he owns the room. As if he *owns me*. And in a way, now he does. I let Danny use me. The thought makes my gaze fall for a moment. I'm going to find a way out of this. I just need time.

My eyes reach Zander's again and his gaze entraps me, as if he knows what I'm thinking. A small voice in the back of my head tells me he can save me. Another calls me a fool, reminding me how Danny *saved* me.

After a moment, I'm forced to look away, my breathing ragged. I can't take looking at him for more than a moment without my heart skipping a beat. It's almost as bad as when I was out there on the auction stage. Disgust twists my stomach as I think about what's happening. I shouldn't be here. This shouldn't be happening.

My skin pricks as I remember seeing Danny in the audience. It took a moment for his eyes to reach mine as I walked off the stage, sold and wanting to run. His eyes seemed to tell me that I was still his, and that no matter whose collar I put on, I only have one Master. My blood chills as I remember that murderous look. It was the same look he gave me in the alley. The look that said if I defy him, I'm a dead woman.

Anxiety threatens to overwhelm me and I bite my lower lip.

Madam Lynn seems to sense my discomfort, and she looks up from my contract, setting her pen aside on the polished cherry wood desk. "Are you all right, Arianna?" she asks gently. I glance at Zander and my heart wobbles again. He's still staring at me. I tear my eyes away and look over at Madam Lynn and shake my head.

"Yes, Madam," I say, lying.

"Are you sure? she asks. "If you have any concerns about the contract you're about to sign, please air them." She pauses to gesture at Zander. "Don't be afraid. You can talk freely in front of Mr. Payne. Anything at all that you want to say."

"I'm fine," I lie again.

Madam Lynn eyes me for a long moment. She senses something that I'm not being upfront about, but she doesn't press the issue. "Don't worry," she tells me gently, offering me a forced smile. "Mr. Payne will let me know if there's anything that needs to be said." She turns to him, waiting for an answer, and something passes between them, although I'm not sure what.

"Mr. Payne, is there anything you would like to say before we commence signing?"

"No," Zander says shortly, his eyes burning into my face.

It's just one word. But I'm nearly consumed by the sound of his voice. It's so deep, rich, and . . . sexy.

My cheeks burn as I'm filled with shame. I should not be having these thoughts.

I look away from both of them, a feeling of worthlessness descending upon me, a self-loathing that almost brings tears to my eyes.

Madam Lynn looks between the both of us and then nods gently, grabbing the stacks of papers.

"If you would just look over everything before signing," Madam Lynn says. "As we discussed before the auction, you have the option to terminate this contract whenever you wish during its term, but you will forfeit the agreed-upon settlement if you choose to do so." She slides the papers over to me along with her pen. The money. I just need to get the money and give it to Danny. Then I'll be done. It makes me a whore, but I'll survive. I'll live and start over.

I'm hardly able to concentrate as I flip through the pages and go over the details of my contract. I feel so nauseated. I want to hurl as I gaze at the dotted line, my heart pounding in my chest.

I don't have to do this, I try to convince myself. *I can go to the cops.*

"Arianna?" Madam Lynn says softly. "Are you all right?"

The words are on my lips. I almost tell her, *I can't do this.* Instead, I say, "I'm fine." as firmly as I can manage. I already know Danny will get to me if I don't go through with this. He has wealth and power, and I have nothing.

Sucking in a deep breath, I close my eyes and quickly scribble my signature over the dotted line.

Madam Lynn gives me a tight smile when I'm done, taking the papers and pen and then sliding them over to Zander.

Zander slowly takes the papers and pen from Madam Lynn. I watch as if I'm not really here, as if it's not real, as he signs each dotted line that requires his name.

I shift in my seat, my skin pricking, my heart racing at the fire that burns in his eyes.

And as he signs the last line that requires his signature, I feel absolutely sick to my stomach.

Like I just signed my soul away to the devil.

CHAPTER 9

ZANDER

I stare at her from across the table, the door closing with a gentle click as Madam Lynn leaves the two of us alone in the conference room. It's rather small compared to the luxury of Club X. But I suppose its only purpose is for signing contracts, so the plain white walls and simple necessities are all that are needed. In here, there's no fantasy or illusion required. It's all business.

Arianna's head falls into a bow and she stays eerily still in her chair. Her eyes are focused on the floor. A darkness in me stirs with delight at her immediate submission to me. It's wrong to think that way and I ignore it, shoving it down and pretending it doesn't exist.

"Arianna," I say her name for the first time. It feels forbidden, too sweet to taste. The syllables linger in the air as she slowly raises her chin, her head still bowed slightly as her gorgeous eyes stare into mine. Deep into me, as if she can see through me.

"What are you doing?" I ask her, taking the attention off me and back onto her lush lips. They're on the pale side, but a soft pink. Her makeup is soft and only there to emphasize her natural beauty.

"Whatever you wish, Sir." I nearly groan at her response. I'm not into power play in the bedroom. I have enough of it throughout the day to fulfill those needs. But she tempts me. It's the look in her eyes that tells me she needs what I can give her. She needs to be dominated, but not like this.

"May I call you Sir?" she asks me in a delicate voice that begs me to take her.

Her soft voice and perfect submission call to me. But I'm not interested in rules and games. The stakes in this game are much too high to play.

It hits me then, with her question, that she's mine. That I can do with her as I please. My dick hardens in my pants just thinking about the sweet sounds that would pour from her lips. I keep my back straight as I adjust my cock to keep it from pressing against the zipper.

I'd love to get lost in her lush curves and bury myself deep inside her. But this is business. And the desires I have aren't right. I tear my eyes away from her and look at the clock on the far wall. The second hand moves slowly, not a single tick audible as it moves seamlessly across the face. Counting time. That's what I'll be doing over the next month. That's all this is.

She's just another woman. My right hand sitting on the table balls into a fist at the thought, knowing it's not true. I rap my knuckles against the table. The steady tapping fills the room as I realize how fucked this situation is.

She's not just another woman. This would be too easy if she were. I wouldn't have come here if it were true.

"Do you know why I bid on you?" I ask her as my eyes lift to her heart-shaped face.

"Because you wanted me to obey your every wish," she answers in a gentle voice, the last word hanging in the air as I stare at her. *Yes*, a voice in the depths of my depravity calls out, begging me to take her as she offered. To give in and simply enjoy her.

"Do you know your Master offered you to me?" I ask her, although it's not really a question. I shouldn't have told her, but I want her to know, I want to see her reaction even more.

"Because my Master owes you?" she asks in a voice that doesn't show what she's feeling. It's all a cognitive process, with no emotion involved. She's hiding it from me.

"Yes, because your prick of a boyfriend owes me." I'm intentionally cold, wanting a response, and she gives it to me.

Her eyes whip to mine and her lips press into a hard line. For a moment, anger rises inside me at the thought of her defending him, but her words cut through it, silencing it.

"He's not my boyfriend." As soon as the words are spoken, her posture returns to what it was.

More than her submission, her anger and her determination that she doesn't belong to him make me want her that much more. Because she doesn't have any claim to him anymore. *Now, she's mine.*

I haven't wanted anyone like this in a long damn time. Maybe not ever. It must be the forbidden aspect of it, the dark desires I've only ever observed from a distance. My eyes glance over her face, waiting for more from her, trying to determine what it is about her that's forcing my hand and only making me want her with more desperation as every minute passes.

She's a siren. Luring me to a depth that already has me making mistakes.

She's the reason I'm in this mess. I *felt* for her. This business isn't about emotions.

I rest my elbow on the table and lean forward, the legs of my chair scooting across the floor and making a screeching noise.

"Can I trust you?" I ask her, finally feeling a hint of a smile reaching my lips.

"Yes, Sir."

"Don't call me Sir," I immediately say, and my command comes out sharp, but she doesn't flinch. My harsh manner doesn't affect her in the least.

"What would you like me to call you?" she asks in an even voice, perfectly still.

I let out a heavy sigh and sit back in my chair. My ankles cross as I look back at her.

"My name is Zander, and you can call me that."

Her lashes flutter as she nods her head and answers obediently, "Yes, Zander."

"I don't really like . . . the lifestyle," I tell her, that smile apparent as I start to spin a beautiful web, something to distract her maybe, something to hide behind. "As a kink, I understand it. But I'm not interested in having a slave or a twenty-four seven power exchange."

Her posture relaxes slightly. "What do you like?" she says, and as she asks me the question, she licks her lips in a nervous manner and clears her throat, setting her clasped hands on the table. Her own mask is crumbling into pieces, and her true emotions are showing. Her voice is lowered and flat.

She's nervous, unhappy even. I'm taken aback for a moment. I hadn't expected this reaction.

"What do you think I like?" I ask her in return. My eyes travel over every one of her features, waiting for more information on her. Everyone has a tell, and I can spot a lie from even the most deceitful men.

"I'm not sure, to be honest." She swallows again and stares at her hands as she fidgets and pinches her fingertips. "I know I'm here to pay a debt. And that you'll use me," she adds and closes her eyes and takes in an uneven breath to steady herself. The smile falls from my face completely.

"I won't do a damn thing to you that you don't want. Let's make that clear right now." My firm voice makes her open her eyes. They're glassy with tears and something else, distrust.

"I promise you. If you don't want me in the least, you can walk through that door and this all ends."

"He'll—"

"He won't do a damn thing to you. Daniel Brooks owes me money. You don't owe anyone."

"I owe him." She breathes the words, her face a reflection of nothing but pain. "I do." Arianna starts to say something, but she doesn't finish. I feel my forehead scrunch as I try to figure out what the hell she's getting at. And then it hits me.

"If you don't want me, you can simply leave." The words, *I'll forgive the debt and you'll be free* are on my lips, but a hiss of a whisper in the darkest part of my mind pleads with me to wait for her reply.

"I do want you," she says, and her gorgeous eyes stare into mine again, piercing through me and threatening to learn every secret I hold.

I want to tell her to leave, to get rid of her. She already has too much power over me. She makes me weak. She makes me foolish. *But she wants me.* And I can't deny I crave the idea of her submitting to me.

"You're going to do everything I say." I don't think as I speak, another side of me taking over.

"Yes, Zander."

"We'll start tomorrow at six in the evening," I tell her, looking straight ahead and past her. My eyes focus on a small dimple on the white wall. An imperfection in the otherwise spotless facade of the conference room.

"What . . . what will you require?" she asks with slight hesitation.

"Whatever I want," I answer her simply. It's not the answer she wants, but she nods her head, her eyes focused on a dark knot in the center of the hard wood table.

"Until tomorrow," I say easily, although not a damn thing in me is relaxed.

"Until tomorrow," she repeats in merely a whisper.

As she walks away, I find myself watching the sway of her hips and imagining taking her over and over. She turns to look over her shoulder one last time, her hand gripping the edge of the door. She licks her lower lip once, drawing my eyes to that beautiful mouth of hers. She starts to say something, but I can't hear her.

"Speak louder," I say, and my voice reverberates off the walls. She startles slightly and lowers her head.

"I just said thank you." Her eyes don't meet mine as she says the words with an uneven cadence. The need to comfort her makes me grip the table harder, keeping me in place.

I nod my head once, watching her face as I dismiss her. "I'll see you tomorrow."

She leaves quietly this time, not looking back at me or meeting my gaze. It's only when she's left that I feel like I can breathe. It's also when I realize how fucked I am.

How Brooks paid his bills isn't any of my damn business. I never should have gone to that fucking auction.

I could have made an example of him and spared Arianna, such a sweetheart, so undeserving of this.

I made a mistake. And I know exactly why.

It's because of *her*. The temptation of having her, of owning her . . . I caved to it.

I don't trust her. But I'll be damned if I don't want her.

CHAPTER 10

ARIANNA

Yes, because your prick of a boyfriend owes me.

Zander's biting words run through my mind as I turn over in my bed, a stream of early morning sunlight peeking through the blinds of my window. His words make me feel like a pawn. An object to be moved around on a chessboard and discarded when no longer useful.

I wrap my arms around my chest tightly, trying to ward away that worthless feeling that keeps threatening to suffocate me.

Madam Lynn's words come back to me. *You have the option to terminate this contract whenever you wish.*

Even Zander told me that I could leave if I didn't want him. But I didn't take the out he offered, and I'm ashamed. My skin pricks from the swell of emotion in my chest.

If I leave Zander, Danny will have me back. I'm a coward for hiding behind another man. Especially in this way. But knowing I'm temporarily his gives me time and protection. My eyes stray over to my canvas. Painting almost always gives me solace when I'm stressed or feeling down. After stretching, I roll out of bed and ready my brushes and colors. I'm not even in the mood to go get coffee. I just want to paint and get lost in the art, forget about everything. I only get a few strokes done before the door opens behind me.

"Ari?" asks Natalie tentatively. It's odd, being in an apartment around someone normal when the reality of my life is nothing like hers. I don't fit in. I never have. I was always trying but never succeeding. I suppose it doesn't matter anymore. I turn around to see her standing in the doorway, still dressed in her pink polka dot pajamas, her hair tousled, peering at me with a grin on her face. "Yes, cavewoman?" I joke halfheartedly, mostly to try to hide my feelings, to pretend everything's all right. Natalie lets out a snort. "Cavewoman? Have you looked in the mirror lately? You're not exactly Cleopatra when you just roll out of bed either."

I huff out a mirthless chuckle. "Can't argue with that."

"Anyway, hater," Natalie says as she pulls her phone out of her pajama pocket, waving at me excitedly as she walks into the room, "you have *got* to see Sarah's ankle! She just got this tattoo done, and I love it!"

"Let me see." I wipe my hands on the cloth I use to clean up with and take the phone from her hands to take a look. It's a picture of a black rose on her ankle. It's super realistic, but it only reminds me of the rose I held yesterday as I was sold.

Natalie grins at me as I stare at the photo. "Do you like it? I think it looks awesome." She taps her finger to her cheek, her expression turning thoughtful as I try to will the memory away and return to just pretending. "I'm thinking about getting the same one, but maybe on my wrist. And I was wondering if you wanted to be the one to do it?"

I don't immediately respond, my eyes still focused on the image of the rose.

"Ari?" Natalie presses, her voice filling with worry. "What's wrong?"

I tear my eyes away from the image to see the concern in Natalie's eyes. A part of me wants to tell her everything. About Danny. About the auction. Zander. But I ignore that part. I don't want to drag her into this, so instead I just say, "Danny and I aren't getting along right now." I'm unable to keep the frustration I feel with my situation from seeping into my voice. Natalie gazes at me with worry. "What's wrong? Did something get out of hand again?"

It sure fucking did.

It hurts me not to tell Natalie the truth. She's been my only friend for the longest time, and she's the only person I have left that I fully trust. But I know deep down that telling her will do more harm than good.

I pass back her phone. "Not really. I just think we need a break from each other."

Natalie slips her phone back into her pocket and places her hands on her hips. "Come on, I know you're not telling me everything. Something got out of hand again and you just don't want to admit it."

Oh, Nat, it's much, much worse than that, I think darkly.

"It's fine," I lie, hating myself for it. "I'm okay. Don't worry."

Natalie's frown deepens. "You're lying to me."

I don't know how to respond. I can see that she cares so much about me. She knows about my troubled past and all of what I went through, and she just doesn't want to see me hurt. But I don't know how to tell her without making things worse.

Right then, my cell buzzes on the nightstand.

I tell Natalie, "Hold on a sec," as I walk over to it, grateful for the interruption. It's a text message from Zander.

> *My driver will be at your apartment at 5:15 to pick you up.*
>
> *The event is black tie. Wear a gown if you have one.*
>
> *Be ready,*
>
> *Z*

"What was that?" Natalie asks, walking over, but I stick my phone back into my pocket before she can ask to see.

"Nothing," I reply, walking back over to my canvas while feeling like total shit for having to lie. "Just some dumb prick texting the wrong number."

CHAPTER 11

ZANDER

I admire punctuality. It says something about a lack of respect when a person is late. I half expected Arianna to be late for Marcus, my driver.

The cufflinks clink as I pick them up off the dresser and slip them into place, locking them and pulling down my sleeves slightly. I straighten my tie as I stare at myself in the mirror. I've always felt comfortable in a tux, but not today. Everything feels tight and suffocating.

I haven't given her a single reason to respect me, but she at least respects the contract.

It's obvious she doesn't want to do this, but I'll give her enough to desire at least a business relationship with me.

Tonight will be dinner, an interview in a way. That's all a dinner really is, just an interview.

I check my phone on the dresser, the dim light brightening the dark bedroom, and see that the photographers will be there to catch a candid shot. I'll pretend I don't see them, just like I always do. I huff a humorless laugh at the ideal headlines PR is looking for.

Eligible Bachelor Falling Head Over Heels.

Love at First Sight for the Family Heir.

I can woo her. I'll get the photographs I need to create the image I want. I don't know how much I'd like to tell Arianna. My gut tells me to be truthful, to have her in on the charade. But the very thought of trusting her makes me panic.

I trust no one. But I can give her enough to go on.

The only loose end is Daniel Brooks.

My phone pings just as I set it back on the dresser. *Charles.*

I read the text silently and then pull back, running my fingers through my hair and slicking it back some before ruffling it in a way that looks careless. I take my time with it, making sure it looks just right.

Charles will take care of Brooks. I only need him to keep an eye on things for now. To make sure he stays in place until I figure out how to handle this.

Ideally, I can convince Arianna to keep the money for herself. The thought of Brooks's face when he finds out . . . how his expression will fall and that cocky glint in his eye will vanish.

But first, the interview. I need to know who she is and what she really wants. A background check can only tell you so much about a person, even one as in depth as what I received. *Don't disappoint me, Miss Owens.*

"She won't." The words slip past my lips as I shrug on my jacket. They hang in the air of my dark bedroom, holding a threat. I'd better be right about her.

My phone pings again, causing a spike of annoyance to run through me, and this time it's Marcus, right on time with Arianna in tow.

I quickly make my way to the front doors, my strides so fast that I create a breeze as I climb down the stairs.

I breathe out a heavy exhale as I unlock the door, swinging it open and preparing for another evening of playing the role I was born into.

The moment I lay eyes on Arianna, the negative air that practically smothers me day in and day out dissipates into the chill of early spring. Marcus is holding the door open for her, one of her small hands in his as her slender legs step out of the car one at a time, her heels clicking on the driveway. It's something about her expression that catches me off guard. Maybe it's the subtle way she brushes her gown and tucks a strand of her hair back as she stands tall and takes in a deep breath.

She's as stunning as ever. I don't know what it is about her. She's not overly sexual, and there's not a single thing I can pinpoint that makes her exceptional. But every time I see her, my world pauses for only a moment, a single point in time where everything stands still, the air in my lungs halting and my heart slowing. There's a quality of innocence and sadness about her that makes me crave something I've never felt before.

I wish I could ignore it.

Her eyes widen when she sees me standing in the doorway staring back at her, and the smile I loathe creeps up and into place, but this time it feels different.

It's an odd thing that I've noticed. Everyone looks at me the same. Their eyes travel up and down my clothing, taking in the details. Businessmen before a board meeting, lower-level thugs at the corner of the street with information, even the vixens that wait late at night at the bars or casinos, hoping to sink their bright red nails into me for a piece of the money. They all look at me the same. Judging, assessing. I can practically see the wheels turning. Some are faster than others, but all of them have telltale signs of what they think.

Arianna is different. The expression on her face tells me she wants me, not my money. The lust turns her eyes glassy and makes her breathing come in short gasps as her eyes linger down my body. But rather than traveling back up to meet my gaze, she turns slightly away as the door closes and she thanks Marcus, her soft voice carried away by the gentle gust of the wind. It makes her hair blow, exposing more of her bare shoulder as her skirt clings to her right side.

When she looks back up, she doesn't meet my gaze.

"Miss Owens," I say loudly enough for her to hear as I walk down the three steps to greet her. I make sure the charming smile is on my face as I wrap my arm around her small waist and plant a chaste kiss on her cheek. Surprise lights her eyes and she doesn't respond for a moment. I don't know what she expected, but I'll surpass anything she's ever experienced. I'll make her want me. Want *this*. She'll play the part so well because I'll make her believe it.

"Mr. Payne." Her voice says my name in a sensual way that's seemingly unintentional.

"Just a moment, Marcus," I tell my driver as he stands by the car. Marcus nods once. He's an older man, maybe in his sixties, but lean and cut from constantly working out. He takes pride in himself and what he does. He's always worked for me, ever since I was sixteen or so. I didn't trust him for years though. After all, it was my father who hired him. But on several occasions, he's proven his loyalty to me and that he can keep secrets.

Still, I'd rather him not hear what I have to tell Arianna. He may be trustworthy, but that doesn't mean I have to take an unnecessary risk. I haven't even confided in Charles. The fewer people who know, the better.

I lean in a bit closer to Arianna, whispering in her ear as I splay my hand along her lower back and lead her into the house. "We need to leave for dinner shortly, but I wanted a private word inside."

"Yes, Si–Zander." Arianna's posture stiffens at her mistake, and I almost regret my plan . . . *almost*.

The moment we're inside, I shut the door and turn to her, slipping my hands into my pockets.

"I'd like you to be my girlfriend," I tell her simply.

She turns on her heels to face me, a look of not understanding on her face. "I'm sorry?" she asks.

I let out a charming chuckle and walk the few steps to be closer to her. The house is so much warmer than outside, so much more welcoming.

"You heard me," I say and take her hands in both of mine. "I'd like you to be my girlfriend in place of what's written in the contract."

A knowing look flashes in her eyes, and those beautiful lips part as understanding shows in her expression. Again, she doesn't respond like I thought she would. "A *fake* girlfriend?" she asks softly.

I pull away slightly and shrug as I reply, "I've never had one, so I'm not sure if it'd be all that fake." My words are casual but calculated. I want her to believe in it. Of course it's fake. Yet another mask to hide behind.

Those dark green eyes pierce through me, not fooled by my tone in the least.

I ignore her prying gaze and the disappointment on her expression. "You'll be my girlfriend. Starting tonight, with a dinner date." I plaster a fake-ass smile on my face and wait for her reaction.

"Yes, Zander." Her posture stiffens now that she knows the rules of this game. It's an act and she's ready to play the part. But I don't want her to just play. I need it to feel real.

"Would you talk that way to your boyfriend?" I ask her. My jaw clenches at the thought of her speaking to Brooks like that. I ignore the jealousy creeping up my spine and sending a chill over every inch of my skin.

Arianna holds her clutch in both of her hands clasped in

front of her and shakes her head slightly. "No," she answers honestly.

"Well then, it's just Zander, all right?" I tell her with a feigned casualness. "None of that . . ." I don't finish, not sure how to word her normal submission.

"I don't know how to . . ."

"How to what, sweetheart?" The little nickname parts from me without my conscious decision, but the way she reacts makes me want to say it a million times over. The soft curves of her face brighten and a beautiful pink hue rises to her cheeks. She lowers her head a little, closing her eyes and sinking her teeth into her bottom lip as she shakes her head slightly.

"How to," she starts to say with her eyes still closed and then opens them slowly, those gorgeous green eyes staring straight into me. The way only she can. "How to act tonight?" she asks in a voice so genuine, so sweet. Fuck, and all because I called her sweetheart? The shift in her is addicting. I love the smile. The light that I give her.

This is why I can't deny her.

CHAPTER 12

ARIANNA

My heart feels like it's going to escape out my throat as I walk up the steps to Gargano's Italiano restaurant, my heels clicking against the stamped concrete. Wonder courses through my limbs as my eyes take in the gorgeous setting, the bright backlighting illuminating the entire area with a soft golden light.

I grip the railing as I walk beside Zander, his arm wrapped loosely around my waist. The stairway leads up to double doors that are surrounded by huge white Greek columns. There's a ten-foot male statue fountain halfway up the steps, the columns of water spraying high into the air. Surrounding the stairs is lush green landscaping, sprinkled with well-manicured walkways and white stone benches.

This is beautiful.

I'm so enthralled with the picturesque scenery that I only make it a couple of steps before I nearly trip over my dress. He told me to wear a gown, and this is the only one I had. The strapless chiffon fabric is forgiving and doesn't wrinkle, which is a plus, but it's a bit long for my petite stature.

Shit.

Zander quickly tightens his powerful arm around my waist, saving me, pulling me against his hard body and forcing me upright. The smell of his masculine cologne tickles my nose as I suck in a grateful breath, my skin pricking from the heat emanating from him. He smells like a fresh breeze and sandalwood. It's both calming and intoxicating.

"I'm sorry," I apologize softly from beneath lowered lashes, my face burning red with embarrassment. "I wasn't watching where I was going."

Zander told me to act like his girlfriend, but all I'm succeeding at is being awkward. I've never done this before, and my insecurity doesn't help. I feel like I'm not worth being on his arm, like it's obvious this isn't real. But I force a smile, trying to keep up appearances.

Zander smiles back at me, moving his hand to my hip, and despite my nervousness, I can't help but notice how handsome he is. He fucking *owns* the black tux and bow tie he's wearing. I've seen many men in expensive suits at Club X, but I've never seen anyone wear one like he does. He radiates, power, wealth, and sex like the sun radiates light. I'm breathless, being this close to him. Like I'm drowning. And I don't want to come up for air.

He chuckles as he says, "I've got you. I won't let you fall." It's an odd thing, seeing how charming he is. I wasn't expecting him to be like this after the signing. I didn't expect any of this. And I don't know how to react.

"This place is beautiful," I say when I catch my breath. I'm trying so hard to be polite and act normal.

"If you think this is beautiful, wait until you see inside," Zander boasts. His teeth sparkle when he smiles. It's a beautiful look on him, that gorgeous smile, but it makes me feel uneasy.

Keeping a firm hand on my waist, he leads me up the stairwell. I raise my head, trying to look regal and confident on his arm.

As soon as we walk in, my breath catches in my throat as I take in the impressive architecture. Soft music plays over unseen speakers, setting the romantic ambience. We pass under impossibly high ceilings with massive archways that are decorated with silk sheers. I can see our reflections in the gleaming marble floors, and gorgeous intricate designs are inlaid across the surfaces.

The walls are painted a soft golden color and the sconces on the wall give off a warm, fuzzy glow, infusing the room with an angelic radiance.

Tables are set with pure white cloth and the china and glasses are accented with gold. *Expensive*. This place looks fucking expensive.

And the people. Everyone here is dressed in their finest.

"You're right," I murmur, feeling extremely insecure. I lack the confidence of the other women around me. I have to look out of place on Zander's arm. "It is better."

Zander winks at me as we walk up to the reservation area, his arm resting possessively on the curve above my ass. "Told you." Seeing his playfulness eases my anxiety somewhat, though I clutch at him tightly to deal with my frazzled nerves.

Not a minute passes before a uniformed waiter walks up to us.

"Do you have a reservation?" the waiter asks, his vest bunching slightly as he stands at the podium, flipping over a sheet of paper.

"Payne," Zander replies shortly, although his voice doesn't hold an edge.

The waiter looks down at the booklet on the podium before nodding and motioning us out of the foyer. "Of course. Right this way, Mr. Payne."

As we follow the waiter and pass by rows of occupied tables, Zander tightens his grip on my waist and pulls me even closer, causing my skin to flush. It's like he wants to show me off to the world and wants everyone to know we're together. I even see a few women look our way, their eyes glued to Zander and traveling down his body, but then stopping at his hold on me.

I try to act confident, but I can't keep my eyes from nervously darting about. I feel like everyone knows I don't belong here. That I'm a worthless fraud.

"Remember to play your role," Zander says under his breath. "Act like you know me and not like you're a scared little doe lost in the woods." He whispers the words, but there's a playful smile still on his lips. His words have an immediate effect on me, and without even thinking, I gently place my hand on his stomach, feeling the hard ridges of his abs beneath his silk dress shirt.

"That's better," he says quietly.

I feel awkward as shit doing it, but I still like it.

We're led to a plush booth at the back of the restaurant. We pass what has to be a VIP section since the tables are more intimate, with lower lighting. I try not to look their way as Zander helps me into the booth before taking his seat.

"What will you have to drink?" the waiter asks while dropping menus in front of us and finishing up what felt like a speech about the fish of the day and something else. I can't concentrate on what he's saying with how fast my heart is beating.

"A white Zinfandel, and I'll have a whiskey sour," Zander replies, not even bothering to ask me what I want.

"Of course, Mr. Payne." The waiter nods his head and walks off.

When he's gone, Zander focuses his eyes on me, the intensity of his gaze causing goosebumps to run down my arms. "You look beautiful."

My lips part with surprise as my cheeks flush. They're simple words, but they mean so much when they sound genuine.

"Thank you," I say softly when I can finally manage, lowering my lashes.

"You're welcome," Zander says, giving me that intense look that makes my skin prick.

For a moment, I get lost in his piercing blue eyes, wanting—no, wishing—that this were something more than what it really is.

"Why are we doing this again?" I blurt out suddenly. I bite my tongue after I say it. I wish I could take the words back. I only need to get the money and forget about all of this.

Zander arches an eyebrow. "Doing what?"

I gesture between us. "This . . . pretending . . ." I shift slightly in my seat, feeling so damn uncomfortable. "I just don't understand."

For the first time this night, Zander frowns and it makes me regret my outburst. "I already told you why," he says, keeping his voice low. "I don't want a slave. It doesn't appeal to me."

And playing make-believe does? I want to ask. It's hard to believe a man like Zander not having *needs*. Sexual needs that revolve around power and domination. The thought brings a heat to my core, and I have to sit back in my seat, grabbing the napkin and delicately placing it over my lap.

"I'd rather get to know you first before having you crawl to me on your hands and knees," Zander says quietly.

His words have a clear effect on my body. I'd happily

crawl to him. He must see the flicker of lust in my eyes, and the same is reflected in his. "You'd like that, wouldn't you?"

Right then, the waiter returns with our drinks, saving me from responding. He sets a sparkling wine glass down in front of me and a mixed drink down in front of Zander.

"Are you ready to order, sir?" the waiter asks.

Zander nods. "A medium rare steak with crab cakes for me, and the stuffed lobster for my sweetheart." He says it again. Sweetheart. And a blush grows on my cheeks, heating my face and making me fiddle with the napkin to soothe my nerves.

"Wonderful selections, sir," the waiter says as he scribbles down the order and leaves us.

"What if I were allergic to seafood?" I have to inquire when he's gone.

Zander shakes his head. "I know you aren't. I want to appear that I know exactly what you want, like I've known you for some time. Remember, we're playing a role." He grins. "Besides, I know you'll love what I ordered for you. Promise."

"I'll take your word for it," I say softly, flashing a fake smile as I take in his admission that he knew I wasn't allergic.

"Smart girl." Zander grins as if pleased by my behavior. He takes a sip of his drink, his penetrating eyes glued to my face. He keeps them on me, literally making me squirm in my seat before asking, "Tell me, what do you do in your free time?"

I hesitate for a moment, glancing down into my glass, a slight flush coming to my cheeks. I wonder if he already knows.

"You can tell me," Zander says gently. "I don't judge." I look up at him, searching his eyes for the reason he's asking me, but I come up emptyhanded.

"I work at a soup kitchen, doing work for the homeless," I tell him. "When I'm not working, I like to paint."

"And you were ashamed to tell me that?" Zander asks.

I bite my lower lip. "It doesn't pay well." That's an understatement.

"But does it make you happy?"

I nod. "In some ways. I like helping people. It makes me feel . . . complete."

Zander eyes twinkle as he gazes at me. "I respect that, I really do. And I'd argue that loving what you do is more important than what a job pays."

"Do you really think so? My bills don't." It's a joke, but I sound absolutely serious.

Zander chuckles. "Can't say I can argue with that." Zander arches a curious eyebrow. "And what about your painting?"

I hesitate. I like my artwork, but I'm not sure if Zander will, or anyone else, for that matter. I don't paint it for others. It's only for me.

"I think I have a picture here in my cell somewhere," I mumble.

"Can I see?" he asks, his tone filled with inquisitiveness that makes me want to show him.

I dig out my cell from my clutch and flip through the photos until I find a picture of one of my paintings. It's on the darker side with a woman lying down on a bed while looking out of a small window. It's not some picturesque painting. Not a classic, like a gorgeous landscape of rolling green hills and an azure blue sky. She's haunted by something that keeps her in her room, although I don't know what.

My throat is dry as I pass him the phone, my palm feeling sweaty and my nerves making me nearly regret showing it to him. Zander takes more than a moment to look over it, his eyes moving slowly across the screen before passing my phone back. "That's beautiful, Arianna," he compliments me, a note of respect entering his voice. "You're very talented."

"It's a little . . ." I trail off as I try to think of the right word to defend it before he can question it, but he fills in the word for me.

"Haunting," he says, and his voice is firm. "It's in her eyes."

I nod my head, not trusting myself to respond verbally. "It really speaks to how well you're able to paint emotions. Not everyone can do that."

I blush furiously at his praise, my self-confidence rising several notches. "Thank you," I say softly.

The waiter returns with both of our plates, and I'm shocked to see how quickly time has gone by. The smell of sweet butter and herbs wafts toward me, and my mouth waters.

We're both quiet as the meals are set in front of us, although I notice Zander checking his phone.

"Is everything all right?" I ask him when we're alone again.

He gives me a smile, picking up his utensils and answering, "It's perfect."

CHAPTER 13

ZANDER

I'm rewarded with a small smile as I set my hand on Arianna's thigh as I readjust in my seat in the back of the Mercedes. I wonder if she's ever been treated this way before. It's not so difficult. A sweet gesture here and there, and alone time over a nice meal.

"I had a really nice time," she says so quietly I almost don't hear her. But then she clears her throat and looks up at me through thick lashes and speaks more clearly. "It was more than I expected. Thank you."

But the way she's acting, it's as if she's never been fed. Like she's never been told that she's beautiful.

It's hard to believe it's true.

"Thank you for accompanying me," I tell her as the car slows down in front of her house.

I expected dinner to be filled with uncomfortable silence, but there wasn't a moment that conversation didn't happen easily and naturally. "We have a dinner this weekend as well."

"Another?" she says, and her voice brightens, which forces a small laugh from me.

"Yes, you may find it hard to believe, but I eat almost every day. Sometimes, several times a day." The joke comes out easily and makes her smile. That sweet one that shows she's honestly happy. It warms my chest to know I put it there.

As Marcus stops the car, I'm quick to open my door and wait for his eyes to catch mine in the rearview mirror. I've got her from here. He stays in his seat as the car remains in park and I quickly shut my door and move to hers to help her out.

"I'm excited to do this again," she says with a sweet smile. She brushes a stray strand of hair from her face as the wind blows by and goosebumps grow along her arms. "Thank you . . . again," she says for at least the fifth time, and this time, she rolls her eyes recognizing how absurd it is that she keeps thanking me. If nothing else, Arianna is full of gratitude and not afraid to show it.

"I am as well." I walk her up to her steps and stop, making sure that she knows I have no intention of going in. It's not about sex. I don't want her to feel pressured, and judging by the soft look on her face, she's not in the least.

She turns on the first step and rocks on her heels as she asks, "This weekend?"

I nod my head and answer, "Four days."

"Will I see you before then?" she asks me. There's a flash of hope in her eyes, and I'm not sure if it's because she wants to see me or if she thinks she won't have to be with me again until this weekend.

"I have a good bit of work to do," I tell her, although in the back of my mind, I can't help but to think I'll have time in the evening. Late evening. She could always come and warm my bed.

I brush off the thought, but the hint of disappointment in her voice as she answers, "Oh, okay," makes me want to offer it to her.

Maybe not this week, but next.

"I'll be calling you. And you can do the same if you'd like. I'll message you if I think of anything," I tell her without thinking. I have no fucking reason to call her whatsoever, but just the offer brings that beautiful smile back to her face.

She tucks her hair behind her ear. "I'll call you then," she says and then closes her eyes and shakes her head slightly. "Or you call me. I'll wait," she adds, then nods her head, looking so serious. "I'll wait for you to call me."

A rough chuckle rises up my chest as I lean forward and give her a chaste kiss goodbye. "All right then, sweetheart."

Even in the darkened night, I can see that blush on her cheeks as she turns to go upstairs.

"Oh, Miss Owens?" I call out her proper name, reaching forward and grabbing her hand in mine. "I had a package delivered for you," I say and pull her closer to me, and she doesn't resist my touch. I wrap my arms around her waist, letting them rest on the lower part of her back, dangerously close to her ass.

Although her eyes dart from my cheek up to my eyes, she doesn't push me away. I can see how her chest is rising and falling with quicker breaths now, and I fucking love it. I'm addicted to the way I so easily affect her.

"You did?" she asks with equal amounts of surprise and delight in her voice. The streetlights shine down on her in a way that casts shadows along the soft curves of her face. She looks up at me, and all I can see in her green eyes is sincerity. I could get lost in the swirls of deep jade that shine back at me.

"I did," I say before I quickly kiss her lips. The kiss is soft and easy, and I need to keep it that way.

It was only one night. An evening just to get to know her, just an interview, but I can feel it turning into something more. A desire for something I shouldn't want.

The reminder of why I'm holding her in my arms, why all of this is even happening is enough to break the spell of her hopeful gaze.

She's temporary. And a mistake I'm merely trying to fix. The knowledge makes my smile slip, but it's instantly replaced by the one I hate.

"I'll see you this weekend." I deliver another small kiss

to the tip of her nose and step out of her embrace. She doesn't seem to notice my change in demeanor. "If you need anything in the meantime, you'll let me know."

"Of course," she replies and bats her eyes, moving the clutch from one hand to the other. "Really, and truly. Thank you for tonight, Zander." Her voice is so full of happiness that I find my reasons for leaving so quickly disappearing into the dark night. But she turns from me before I can go back to her, her hips swaying and taunting me as she walks closer to the front door and grips the railing.

As I watch her walk up the steps, those gorgeous curves tempting me as the soft sounds of the night air swish by and make her dress cling to her, I finally answer her beneath my breath. "My pleasure, sweetheart."

CHAPTER 14

ARIANNA

My pleasure, sweetheart.

Zander's words linger in my mind as I step into my shared apartment and gently close the door behind me, feeling a heavy mix of emotions coursing through my chest. Zander has been such a gentleman. It was so unexpected that I don't know how to process it. It's hard not to feel butterflies, even knowing it's all fake.

I suck in a heavy breath, remembering how it felt to be held in his arms at the end of dinner. Zander made me feel special, like I was the only woman in the room. And even though I felt unworthy to be there with him, I wanted it to be real. I wanted desperately to think that he truly wanted me beside him.

It felt like that. It felt *real*.

I run my finger down the side of the package that was left for me. It's not hard to imagine that it's a dress for this weekend. The white box is large, yet light. My heart beats with anticipation to open it.

I spin around when I hear Natalie's shocked voice.

"Jesus, Ari, what are you dressed up for?" She walks into the living room and adds, "You look beautiful!"

Natalie's in her favorite pair of pink polka dot pajamas, a half-finished cup of Greek yogurt in her hand, her jaw hanging slack. The television's on and running in the background, playing some rerun of one of the *Real Housewives* reality TV shows she likes to watch.

She sets her yogurt down on the end table next to the couch and walks over to inspect my dress.

My tongue is tied. I don't know how to tell her the truth. It all feels . . . dirty. "I was out with a friend," I lie.

Natalie studies me suspiciously. "What sort of friend? And since when do you go out dressed like that for *a friend?*" Although she's practically interrogating me as she crosses her arms, she has the hint of a smile playing on her lips.

I'm unable to answer her question. The butterflies fluttering in my stomach want to tell her about tonight. About dinner and how Zander treated me, but it's not real and it'll only complicate things to involve anyone else. Plus, I'm not sure what I'm allowed to reveal given the non-disclosure agreement I signed at Club X. I really wish she would stop prying. It puts me in such an uncomfortable position. She peers closely at me when I don't answer right away. "And what's this . . ." her voice trails off as if she realizes something. "Wait a minute . . . you weren't out there with Danny, were you? Is that why you don't want to tell me what's going on? 'Cause you told me you were taking a break with him, and you're really not?" Her voice raises and the smile vanishes.

I roll my eyes at where her mind goes, holding the package a bit closer to me. I wish it were that simple.

Natalie persists, insisting, "I know you were with someone. I can smell cologne on you."

"It wasn't with Danny," I say.

Natalie presses. "Who then?"

I grit my teeth, wishing I didn't have to do this. "I can't say. Just a friend."

Natalie scrunches her face into a frustrated scowl. "You know what? Your sudden secretive ways are really starting to get to me."

I let out a sigh. "I'm sorry, Nat. I just don't want to say anything right now."

Natalie places her hands on her hips. "Well, when will you be able to say anything then? The suspense is killing me." She lightens the mood by exaggerating her last line and moving to snatch her cup of yogurt up again.

I remain tight-lipped. "I don't know. Soon."

Natalie stares at me for a long moment before letting out a resigned sigh and taking a spoonful of yogurt. "Okay. I'm going to let you off the hook for now. But can you promise me one thing?"

I'm on edge. "What?"

"Don't see that piece of shit Danny ever again, pretty please?"

"He's not a piece of shit," I say reflexively. I don't know why I say that. Everything Danny has done to me recently leading up to the auction says he is. And after what Zander told me, I should never want to see him again. But no matter how hard I try, I can't get over what he did for me.

He saved me. I really wanted to kill myself. I would have if he hadn't stopped me.

Natalie's jaw drops. "Are you kidding me? He beat the hell out of you for the past couple of months, and now you're defending him? What the hell is wrong with you?"

God, I don't want to fight. I toss the package down feeling like I'm in a no-win situation. But it's a tight spot that I put myself in. I seriously want to go into my room and curl up into a little ball. "Please, Nat," I plead. "I'm tired and don't want to talk about this right now."

Natalie stares at me long and hard before finally shaking her head. "Fine. But I don't think I'll ever understand this relationship you have with him, and I don't think I ever want to." My throat feels tight as I take in her words. I didn't ask for her support, and I understand that she doesn't like it, but it still hurts. "I'm going to bed. Don't forget to turn the lights off."

She disappears down the hall, leaving me alone.

I suck in a heavy breath as tears sting my eyes, my gaze going down to the package sitting on the sofa. I feel like crap having to lie to Natalie, but I don't know what else I can do.

Sighing, I slump down on the couch, running my fingers over the package.

I tear it open and stare in shock at what's inside. It's a beautiful gown, a white, sparkly number with glittering rhinestones that shimmer like diamonds. I run my fingers over the exquisite tailoring, thinking that it's the nicest gift anyone has ever given me.

But just like tonight, just like the butterflies in my stomach, it's a lie.

I cover the dress up with the thin piece of white tissue paper and let my head fall back against the sofa.

None of this is real, and I need to protect myself and remember that.

CHAPTER 15

ZANDER

I turn down the radio as I pull off the highway heading down to Arianna's place. It's nearly eight on a Friday, but it's the only night I can make time for her.

My turn signal clicks as I turn onto her street and remember the article in the paper this morning. It's nothing huge, and I doubt Arianna's read it. The picture of her is perfect, capturing the moment and sending the message that I'm no longer on the market. She may never even know about it unless she searches her name or someone points it out to her.

I want to be the one to show her. I can't wait to see her reaction when she sees. Although it does say, "mystery woman." The next one will have her name. I made sure of that.

I pass a row of condominiums. I hate this area in the city. The brick is old and worn, and graffiti covers half the buildings. She doesn't belong here. I grip the steering wheel tighter as I park out front of her building and look up to her apartment window. The lights are on.

It's a weird feeling, something like nervousness as I pull out my phone. It doesn't make sense, and I ignore it as I text her that I'm outside. I stare up to her window, waiting for a response. I let out a small laugh as I see her pull the curtains back to look outside.

The phone pings as I open my car door, and I glance at it to see what she's said as I jog up the stairs. *Come on up.*

My heart flutters as I walk into the warmth of the building and see her standing in her open doorway.

"Hi," she says sweetly as she opens the door wider and bites her lower lip.

Her nightgown looks nothing like what I'd expect on her. It's a simple cotton thing, so thin that I can see the outline of her nipples. It's the colors that I don't expect. Patches of bright and neon colors.

"It's my roommate's," Arianna says, answering the unspoken question. She shrugs slightly before saying, "It's laundry day."

I turn to take her in, and something shifts. The flutters in my stomach turn to stone as she crosses her arms across her chest and avoids looking at me.

That smile I've been thinking about for the past few days, the one that's invaded my every waking moment, is nowhere to be seen.

"How are you?" I ask her out of curiosity as I walk into her apartment.

"Fine, how are you?" she answers with a politeness I've come to expect from her.

"All right." My answer is a bit absent as I glance around her place. I've never seen the inside before. The walls are an off-white, typical in apartments, but there are so many photos on the wall that color the room. On the far wall of the living room, there have to be at least thirty photos, all framed and hung in the shape of a heart above a lime green Ikea sofa littered with pillows in different colors. It takes me by surprise.

"Those are Natalie's," Arianna says and nods toward the living room.

"Ah." I walk in a few steps and lean against the banister.

"I didn't expect you," Arianna says in a way that makes it obvious she's uncomfortable with me dropping by unannounced like this. She tucks her hair behind her ear as she looks past me and back into the living room as she says quietly, "I would have cleaned up." Her entire demeanor has changed since I saw her last. My heart feels heavy in my chest, as if it's falling. It's an unnatural feeling, something I'm not used to.

"I thought I would surprise you," I tell her. "I wanted to make sure you got your dress."

I expect a smile, but instead, she only nods and answers respectfully, "I did, and it's beautiful. Thank you so much."

My heart thuds once, then twice. Maybe this was a mistake. I run my hand through my hair, not knowing what the fuck to do. I don't have a significant other for a reason.

"I'm sorry," Arianna's voice comes out small. "I should have texted you to thank you."

My gaze travels over her entire body. She's uncomfortable, but presenting herself. Just like at the auction. There's a small bit of paint on her elbow, and at first, it looks like a bruise, but it's definitely paint.

"Have you done any more artwork?" I ask her, trying to change the subject. I can't leave her feeling like this. The gala is tomorrow, and I don't trust whatever's going on in her head right now.

She nods her head, a bit of brightness lighting her dark green eyes. It makes my lips kick up into a smirk. "Let me see," I tell her.

"Oh." She takes half a step back and bites her lip. "It's not really done."

My stomach drops at her confession, although she tries to back out of the excuse. "I can still show you," she says apologetically.

"No," I say and wave her concern away. "That's fine. If it's not done, I'll wait."

She nods her head and visibly swallows, awkwardness returning.

"I was just on my way to bed," Arianna says quietly. "I'm just tired, really."

"All right then," I tell her, taking the cue to leave and

feeling like a fucking jackass. "I'll head on out and go home."

She's a smart woman. She knows this isn't real, and whatever connection we had at dinner is long gone. My blood runs cold at the thought. A frown settles on my face and refuses to budge. *How did I fuck this up?* I shake the thought away. There was nothing to fuck up. It was stupid for me to visit her.

I open the door, seeing myself out, but she's quick to follow me. I stand in the open doorway. "I'll be with Marcus around six to pick you up tomorrow."

A small smile slowly grows on her lips, and I'll be damned, but my heart flutters with hope.

"Come here," I say and cup my hand around the back of her head and bring her in for a kiss. My lips press against hers, gently at first, as she tilts her head and holds her body close against mine.

I'm just kissing my sweetheart goodnight.

A spark ignites between us as I deepen the kiss, letting my other hand roam down to her waist and pulling her even closer to me. The tip of my tongue slips between the seam of her lips, and she parts them for me, moaning softly into my mouth and gripping my shirt in her hands. Electricity runs over every inch of my skin, a dark beast inside me coming to life, wanting to hold onto her and not let go.

This is what we had before, and I don't want to lose it. I don't want to take another step away and never have this again.

"Hey." My voice is low as I pull back from the kiss and grip her chin in my hand. Her eyes are still closed, as if she's in a daze. I know I'm not the only one who feels this. "Are you all right?" I need to know. I don't want to lose her again. "Did Brooks message you?" I ask her, even though I know Danny's not bothering her. Charles is still watching him and has his phone tapped. But something's not right with her.

"I'm just not feeling well," she tells me, although her eyes don't hold my gaze.

"Is there something I can get you?"

"No." She pulls away from me, holding the edge of the door, ready to close it. "I'll be all right."

I search her eyes and almost leave it be. I almost let her get away with brushing me off, but something comes over me. I push the door open wider and step back in. Arianna's eyes open wider and she walks backward, letting me invade her space and close the door behind me.

"You're mine, sweetheart," I tell her with a voice I don't recognize. "I need to take care of you." I let the flood of images that have kept me awake at night fuel my desire to keep moving. "Do you want that?" I ask her.

"When's the last time you got off?" I ask her, feeling my dick harden in my pants.

She turns to look behind her, swallowing, and quickly answers, "My roommate—"

"Get upstairs," I cut her off. I know exactly what

Arianna needs, and I'm not going to hold back when I can give it to her.

I follow her up the steps, that lush ass swaying as I unbutton my shirt.

Arianna speaks quietly as she walks in front of me, leading me to her bedroom. "It's just that I'm confused and I don't know how to react to it all." She opens her door and waits for me to walk in before closing it and locking the doorknob.

I don't hesitate to remove my shirt as she turns around. "And . . ." she starts to say, but then pauses mid-sentence as her eyes take me in. My sweetheart definitely knows how to boost my ego.

"I'm your Master, aren't I?" I ask her, taking the two strides to fill the space between us. "I do the worrying," I say as I cup her chin. My thumb brushes along her lower lip as her green eyes search mine.

"You are?" she asks me, her breath coming up short.

"I want to be." I say the words before I know how true they are. "Do you want me to be your Master, sweetheart?"

She nods her head once and whispers, "Yes."

CHAPTER 16

ARIANNA

"You need to get off," Zander says, his voice low and husky, his thumb resting on my lips. I stare into his piercing blue eyes, desire heating my core.

"I–I–I don't think I can," I stammer. I'm starting to feel so very hot, the heat from his hard body causing my temperature to rise, my heart pounding in my chest.

"You can," Zander says firmly. "And you will."

He caresses the side of my face gently, his touch causing my skin to tingle all over. I close my eyes at the sensation, reveling in the feel of his gentle touch against my skin. I want to do as he says. I *want* to please him. But I don't know if it'll be easy. I've always used pain to get my release. And . . .

Danny's words play in my mind.

No matter whose collar you put on, I'm still your Master. And the only one to bring me pleasure is him. I can only have it through pain.

"Danny—" I begin to say. I need Zander to know.

"Isn't your Master anymore," Zander finishes for me. "I am. And I want you to get on that bed, spread your legs wide, and rub your pussy for me."

The intensity of his words causes my pussy to clench, my nipples pebbling against the flimsy nightgown.

Zander says, "You're wet for me already." It's not a question but a statement of fact.

"Yes," I whisper, my pulse quickening, my breathing ragged. My body is still and tense.

Zander's fingers trail back down to my lips. He presses his thumb against them, demanding entry. I part my lips, letting him gently place his thumb on my tongue. "Suck," he commands me.

I do as he says, gently sucking on his thumb exactly how he wants me to. As if it's his cock. I don't close my eyes at first. I watch him and his reaction as I do what I'm told.

A soft groan escapes his lips and he closes his eyes briefly. When he opens them, he pulls his thumb from between my lips, leaving me wanting more, and asks softly, "Would you like to please me?"

Slowly, I nod my head, my clit throbbing. "Yes," I say, my voice barely above a whisper. Maybe I'm weak, but I desperately want to please him.

"I won't allow it," Zander says in his deep voice. My

body freezes until he adds, "Not until you've made yourself cum."

I nod my head and take a step backward, the backs of my knees hitting the mattress. I haven't touched myself in . . . in over a year. I wasn't allowed.

Anxiety mixes with desire as I fall back on my bed and scoot myself back with my knees bent upward. Every move is deliberate, and my eyes stay on Zander's, making sure that he's pleased with everything.

His breathing comes in heavier as he watches me. Zander grabs my desk chair, placing it in front of the bed. His eyes never leave me as he sits down, spreading his legs out wide. I can't help but notice the huge bulge pressing against his dark dress pants, straining to get out.

"Lift your gown," Zander commands, his voice heavy. Husky. "Panties off."

I do as he says, pulling my gown all the way up to my upper stomach and pushing my underwear off. My fingers tremble as they push against my legs. Zander inhales sharply at the sight of me. I wait for him to touch himself, but he doesn't. His hands stay on his thighs.

"Touch yourself," he orders, his voice strained.

Slowly, I run my hand down my stomach and then between my legs. Right before I touch myself, I freeze, anxiety washing over me. I'm not allowed to. I haven't been allowed in so long. *But Danny is not my Master anymore.* Still, it's hard to move forward.

I look at Zander for guidance, fear keeping me from

obeying. "I haven't . . ." I look up at the ceiling before I continue. "I haven't in a long time," I admit.

Anger flashes in Zander's eyes. "You weren't allowed to touch yourself?"

I shake my head. "No. Or cum without . . . pain."

"You have my permission and that's all you need," Zander says, his voice tight. "Touch yourself."

Taking a deep breath, I place the tips of my fingers on my throbbing clit and rub a small circle against it with just a touch of pressure. Warmth flows from my belly outward, running a fire through my body all the way up to my neck. A soft moan escapes my lips as my head lolls to the side, my eyes still on Zander, my Master.

"Good girl," Zander groans.

I slowly move my hand up and down between my folds, and the touch is so foreign to me as my fingers spread the moisture back up to my clit.

"You're gorgeous like this," Zander says softly, the sexy tone of his deep voice causing my limbs to quiver. "You deserve this. Relax and just let go."

Another sigh escapes my lips as I arch my back, lifting myself up with the tips of my toes, and rubbing myself in a circular motion, faster and harder.

"Yes," Zander hisses.

His praise makes me want more. Keeping myself suspended and my back arched, the bed creaks as my ass sways, barely brushing against the bedding.

For a moment, I remember Natalie's home and I'm scared that I might be making too much noise. The last thing I want is for her to hear, but I'm too far gone now to stop. And I don't want to disobey him.

"Fuck," Zander groans. "I'm so fucking hard for you."

"Imagine my cock deep inside you," Zander says, his voice filled with lust, "filling you up."

I moan at his words, the fire raging hotter, rubbing myself faster, all the while staring into Zander's eyes.

"I want you to cum for me," Zander demands.

His command is my undoing. My back arches, and the inferno inside my stomach reaches a crescendo, sending shockwaves of pleasure all over my body. Wave after wave hits me and makes my neck arch, forcing me to look away from Zander. The room spins above me as waves of pleasure continue to radiate from my core and I lose all sense of time.

Zander's standing at the foot of the bed when I come back down from my high.

"On your knees," he commands me even as the dull ache between my legs continues to send shockwaves through me.

I instantly obey him, slipping out of the bed and onto the floor, falling to my knees at Zander's feet. My mouth parts as my pussy pulses and a wave of pleasure spikes through me.

He grips his belt at his waist and pulls it out with one smooth movement, letting the hiss of the leather against the silk fabric fill the room along with the sounds of our heavy breathing. Zander tosses the belt to the floor beside him, but he doesn't make a move, staring down at me expectantly.

My heart pounds as I realize he's waiting for me. I reach up and undo the button of his expensive dress pants and tug on the zipper, pulling his slacks and his underwear down around his thighs with one soft jerk.

I'm nearly slapped in the face as his thick dick springs free. My mouth waters as I look at it swinging back and forth before wrapping my fingers around his shaft. His cock pulsates in my hand, beating in tandem with my pounding heartbeat.

"Suck," he tells me, his voice strained as his fingers spear through my hair.

Slowly, I part my lips, allowing him entry to my mouth. I have to open as wide as I can to accommodate his size as his head gently pushes against my tongue, the sweet tang of his precum making me moan.

"Fuck," Zander murmurs, throwing his head back.

Gripping his shaft with my right hand, I swirl my tongue around his head, teasing it before letting him go further into my mouth.

I rock on my heels as I hollow my cheeks and take more of him into my mouth. He feels like smooth velvet over steel as I press my lips against him. Massaging, sucking, and pleasing him the best I can.

Zander moans again, placing his hands on either side of my head, taking control. He thrusts his cock all the way into my mouth, almost causing me to gag. He pulls out quickly, stroking himself once while I catch my breath. I open wide for him and wait. My hands are on my thighs, and I keep my eyes on his.

"Good girl," he says as he pushes himself back into my mouth. It's difficult, but I hold back my gag reflex as he thrusts deep inside my mouth, his thick head hitting the back of my throat. Zander's breathing quickens as he picks up his pace, holding the back of my head firmly. My eyes sting with the need to breathe, but before it's too much, he pulls out and then does it all again. It takes all of my self-control to not pull away, his huge cock triggering my gag reflex with almost every thrust. But I love it. I want him to take all the pleasure he can from me.

"I'm gonna cum," I hear him groan above me, his breath coming in ragged pants.

His thrusts are short, shallow pumps, but he remains deep in me as I feel his big dick grow impossibly hard in my mouth. *One. Two. Three.*

My fingernails dig into my thighs as he cums in the back of my throat. A strangled gasp escapes Zander's lips on his final thrust.

I swallow everything, taking it all and loving how I made him come undone. When he pulls away from me, I expect him to clean himself up, to leave me where I am and make me wait for him.

But he reaches down, gripping my chin in his hand, and kisses me. I'm caught by surprise, his taste still in my mouth. It's only his lips, but still, I didn't expect it.

He pulls away, his breath still ragged as his eyes search my face.

"Did you enjoy it?" he asks me.

"Yes," I answer immediately.

He releases me, and I instantly miss his warmth. I more than enjoyed it. *I need more.*

❄

I HOPE ZANDER WILL BE PLEASED.

I glance over my appearance in the mirror, my heart skipping a beat at my reflection. It's the next day after our hot foreplay session, and I'm getting ready for another date. Zander's taking me somewhere new tonight. Somewhere important. And I don't want to disappoint him.

I'm wearing the gorgeous white gown made of sparkling rhinestones Zander gave me, my hair pulled up into an elegant French bun with wispy bangs framing my face. I had to watch a video on how to put my hair up like this, but it was worth it.

I hardly recognize myself.

With my dangling diamond earrings, dramatic makeup, and gorgeous gold bracelet, I look like some wealthy debutante. Everything about my appearance says eloquence and beauty, even if the diamonds are fake. Still, I don't *feel* like I'll belong on Zander's arm. I feel like I'm just playing dress-up, hiding the flaws that lie just beneath the surface.

I don't think I can ever match up to the woman who's looking back at me in the mirror. That person I see, I don't recognize her. It's not the real me. I'm just a fraud.

I suck in a breath as I remember his warm lips pressed against mine. I got lost in the moment. Lost in him. I never wanted it to end. Just being around him makes me feel dizzy with euphoria. It's not supposed to be this way. It's just an act. It's all fake.

But why does it feel so fucking real?

Because he's my Master, a voice whispers in the back of my mind. The instant I think the words, my body relaxes.

My pulse races as warmth flows through my chest. I can't get over the way he looks at me. Like I'm *his*. It makes me feel wanted. Even if it is only for thirty days.

I shake off the feeling of anxiety rolling through me, the questions and fear. He'll take care of me. I close my eyes and try to believe it, but I know it's foolish. *This is temporary.*

He's going to be here soon to pick me up.

And I know the moment I see him, I'm going to go weak in the knees. It's what he does to me. He makes me powerless, but I want it. I want to give it all to him.

It scares me.

It makes me feel like I'm drowning.

And I don't want anyone to save me.

CHAPTER 17

ZANDER

The moment the limo pulls up, she's at the door to the townhouse, not making me wait. I should move and get my ass out of the limo to go to her, but I'm struck for a moment. She stands out against the dark red brick of the old building, her white dress brushing against her shapely legs as the wind blows, further emphasizing her tempting curves. She's striking, gorgeous even.

She's all I've thought about since I left her.

The trees and bushes along the sidewalk and in front of her building are barren. The buildings are old and worn. History has been unkind to them. Maybe her past is dark, but I know with everything in me that she doesn't belong here. Not anymore.

The wind is harsh, blowing her shawl and exposing her bare shoulders. She lets out a gasp that I imagine I can hear as she reaches for the edge of her shawl. It's blowing in the wind with the threat of losing it clearly on her face. Although the weather is more like spring than the end of winter, with the wind, I know she must feel the chill.

She grips the iron railing, steadying herself on the landing of the stone steps as Marcus opens his driver's door to the limo. It brings me back to the moment, and I'm quick to get out so I can wave him back.

As my dress shoes slap against the paved sidewalk, my blood heats. She's sure to be noticed tonight, which will bring more attention than usual. That, combined with the news article, I'm sure will get people talking. My nerves prick at the thought. I usually enjoy blending in. The familiar is expected and also ignored.

She certainly isn't familiar, and I know damn well she won't be ignored.

I have to jog to meet her at the bottom of the steps. "You look beautiful," I compliment her as I hold out my hand. A beautiful blush rises to her cheeks as she sets her small hand in mine.

"Thank you," she says, and her voice is small and full of genuine happiness. I don't know what she expects out of this, with me being her Master, but I can take care of her. And I intend to. I've almost messaged Lucian and Isaac a few times to ask what the fuck I'm supposed to do. I'm not going to let on to that fact though.

I hold her hand and open her door for her as a gentleman should. I wait for her to sit back in her seat before closing it and getting in on the other side.

It only hits me when we're alone in the back of the

limo and Marcus pulls away that I'm really taking her to an event. I don't bring guests anywhere. I don't make appearances with any women, and I've never been seen with a significant other. Not that I've had them. A quick fuck to sate my appetite is all I've ever indulged in.

But tonight is different. It's a statement as well.

It's quiet for a moment, and I can see that it's getting to Arianna. Her fingers tangle with one another, and more than once, she parts her lips to say something, chancing a look up at me but then looking back to the floor of the cabin.

I finally break the tension. "I'd like you to do what I say tonight." She needs to be perfect. She needs to play the part well so that no one will question what we are and my image will stay intact.

"Of course," she answers quickly, nodding her head. "I promise I'll do my best *and* it will be good enough."

I eye her and take in the conviction in her voice.

"Have you been to a gala?" I ask her, reaching across the cabin to the champagne that's sitting on ice. I uncork it with a flourish as she answers that she hasn't, but she's fully aware of how she's supposed to act and that she won't disappoint me.

The champagne pops, and the sound of it spilling easily into the first flute is accompanied by the sound of my heart beating in my chest. She continues talking nervously, but she sounds eloquent, even with the nerves evident. She's going to be perfect.

The glass flutes clink against each other as the limo goes over a small bump and I fill the second halfway.

"Champagne?" I offer as I set the bottle back down.

"Thank you," she says and accepts the glass with grace although she doesn't take a drink. I taste mine, the sweetness coating my tongue.

"You're a smart woman, so I'm sure you'll be fine," I tell her as I place my hand on her knee. "You'll be quiet for most of the night and simply stay on my arm."

"Yes," she answers quickly, both of her hands wrapped around the skinny stem of the glass sitting in her lap.

"As far as anyone knows, you're my girlfriend. It's a new relationship." I down the rest of the champagne and set the empty glass into its place, leaning forward and continuing to talk. "We met through a mutual friend if anyone asks, although I'll do my best to do most of the talking."

"Absolutely," she answers firmly.

I nod my head at her and let my eyes travel down her dress. "You really do look beautiful, sweetheart." I don't think about the words until they've left me. A pleasant sound comes from her lips. Not a gasp of surprise or a laugh, but something in-between. As if she's flattered, but that she doesn't believe me.

"I'm proud to have you by my side tonight. Do you know that?" I ask her.

She gazes at me for a moment but doesn't answer quickly, which isn't in her nature. She finally whispers,

"Thank you." It makes me think she truly doesn't believe it. I need to change that.

I scoot closer to her and rest my hand on her thigh as I lean in and whisper against the shell of her ear, "A lot of the women in there are going to be jealous of you tonight."

She turns quickly in her seat to look me in the eyes. "Because they want you?" she asks softly. There's an expression in her eyes I don't recognize, maybe fear, but I'm not sure.

"No," I say, and I can feel my forehead pinch as I continue, "Just because you're so beautiful." Her cheeks stain with that beautiful red and she looks away, pushing a stray strand of hair from her face.

Time passes as we both sway slightly in the limo, the comfortable silence stretching between us. My phone dings, and I'm quick to see who it is. With these functions, there's always someone who wants to ensure they'll be seen talking to me.

I've already missed half a dozen messages and two phone calls, several of which are from my father. I sigh and lean back in my seat, leaving the warmth of her small frame and focusing on work. She scoots closer to me, resting her hand on my thigh and leaning against me. I wait for her to say something, giving her the attention she needs, but she doesn't say a thing. I wrap my arm around her and continue to check my email as she lays her head against me and looks out the window. She's simply happy to be held.

The limo comes to a stop, and it's only when Marcus opens his door that I realize we're here already.

"Wait here," I tell her as she reaches for the door. "I'll get out first, then open your door. You will not slide across the seat. Instead, I want you to wait for me there," I say and nod toward her door.

"I can do that. I *will* do that." She holds my gaze as she answers me, and something flickers between us. She wants to please me. And I know she can. A small smile grows on my face and it's then that I realize I've been more of myself around her than I should have been. I've given her a glimpse behind the mask. Instead of feeling threatened, something else settles in my chest, leaning against my heart for a moment until I hear the rap of knuckles at my door. Marcus is waiting, asking for permission to open my door.

I pull the handle and step out, immediately struck by the bright lights at the front entrance and the sparkle of gowns adorned in jewels from the crowd out front. Many turn to look to see who's arrived. It's show time. I recognize four men instantly, sharing a knowing look between them as they nod my way.

I fasten the middle button of my jacket and turn my back to them as I walk around the limo to open Arianna's door. The conversations continue behind me and another limo pulls up behind us. Waiting.

As I open her door and reach my hand out for her, I know many of them are watching us. My heart hammers against my chest as I question whether I've done the right thing.

If I'd kept her a secret, they'd have thought the worst of me. They would have come to the conclusion that I was just like Brooks. I need them to think otherwise. To believe in the character I've created. Most shouldn't know, but I'm not a fool. All men talk, and these circles are small but well connected.

It's reasonable for them to think that I've had a crush on her. And I'll be playing up that part tonight, starting with the kiss I plant on the back of her hand as she stands on the pavement.

A warm blush travels to her cheeks and she naturally smiles at me, batting her lashes and waiting for me. She's stunning and seems shy. She's acting brilliantly. Playing the perfect role, although the idea that it's an act makes me tense.

I whisper in her ear, "Be good for me." And then I plant a small kiss on her cheek. As I pull away to look into her eyes, something changes in her expression. She's stiff as she nods her head, and I question my decision to be so open.

To me, this is an act. But to her . . . maybe it's something else.

I plant a kiss on her lips, ignoring the spark igniting from the instant touch and wrapping my arm around her waist.

She only breathes once we've made it to the foyer, and even then, she still looks struck with surprise. A good surprise.

If I can keep her like this all night, her presence will

only make me look as though this is a genuine attraction.

I force the smile to stay on my face as my father walks toward me, a stern expression firmly in place as his eyes flicker to Arianna and then back to me.

I part with her for a moment, leaving her at the entrance of the foyer with the whispered words, "Stay here."

She doesn't have time to acknowledge me as I take large steps away from her to meet my father. My father is a loose cannon, and I don't like the way he looks at my sweetheart. And whatever he has to say, it won't be said in front of her. I won't allow it.

My defenses rise as he stops in front of me, talking beneath his breath.

"You brought her?" he asks with an air of disbelief. My expression is like stone, fixed in place. Even the jovial glint in my eyes stays in place.

"Why wouldn't I?" I ask him, feeling the smile on my face.

"From what I've heard, she should be in your bedroom . . . or someone else's." A huff of a laugh rises up my chest as I look away from my father and back to the crowd, turning to look over my shoulder and back to Arianna who's waiting for me patiently.

"Let me get her comfortable," I tell my father. "I'll talk to you later tonight," I say and pat his arm as if it was a pleasant conversation and he finally releases me. I have no intention of speaking to him again tonight. Or tomorrow.

Adrenaline races in my blood as I leave him behind me and walk toward Arianna. The entire crowd is stealing glances at her as I hold out my arm to her. Watching her. Watching *us*.

I do need to find out what he knows, though, how the fuck he found out about her so quickly, and who else is aware of the situation.

And more importantly, I need to figure out where the information came from.

CHAPTER 18

ARIANNA

"Is it hot in here to you?" Dahlia asks, fanning herself with the fancy dinner menu that was given to all the guests in attendance. I tear my eyes away from the throng of people filling the dining room, turning them on Dahlia. I've been busy looking for Zander, who seems to have gotten lost in the crowd. Shortly after arriving, he led me to this table and told me to sit down after quickly introducing me to Dahlia and Lucian Stone.

It's been ten minutes so far, and he's still not back yet.

I pick nervously at my fingernails as I flash her a friendly smile, shaking my head, trying to hide my anxiety. This is yet another place that I feel out of place, a place where wealth and gaudy opulence is on proud display. It was easier with him here with me. All the guests are dressed in finery, and while I'm dressed similarly, I know it's all paid for by Zander. "No, it feels fine to me," I answer her.

Though we haven't spoken much since Zander ran off, I like Dahlia. She's gorgeous with a charismatic charm that makes me feel like I already know her. I've seen her in passing a few times at Club X, but I've never really talked to her before today. And I'm sure as shit not going to bring that up. I hope she doesn't recognize me. I keep stealing glances, and she doesn't seem to make the connection. If she does, she's not judging me.

If she knew the circumstances, I'm sure she would.

I think it's amazing that she's actually married to someone who is her Dom, although I guess it's more of a kink for them than a lifestyle. That's just an assumption though. I know he used to be her Dom. I nervously glance down to my fingers, tangling them as I remember seeing them in the club. I didn't know it was *him*, but I recognize her.

Lucian's been nothing but gracious to his wife. I glance over at him, noting how smooth he looks in his dapper tuxedo. He's a handsome man, and part of his personality reminds me of Zander's. Looking out into the crowd, he has an aura of power about him.

"Oh," Dahlia mutters, fanning herself fervently and wiping at her brow. I love the dress she's wearing, a white lace number that's provocative yet chaste. She practically glows in it. "I'm burning up."

As if summoned by her complaint, a male waiter in uniform shows up at her side with a tray of ice-cold drinks. They're made with a soda base, but that's all I can tell from the small bubbles on the glass and the ones still clinging to the crushed lemons and limes at the bottom of each.

"Would you care for a refreshment?" he asks us, offering the tray.

I expect Dahlia to down the cold beverage immediately, but she looks at the drink warily. "Is there alcohol in this?" she asks the waiter with her head tilted slightly.

The waiter, a young blond man with charming dimples, smiles and replies cheerfully, "It's the signature cocktail for this evening. Citrus vodka and Sprite."

Dahlia immediately shakes her head vigorously. "Oh no, thank you though. May I have a glass of water please?"

"Of course." The waiter nods his head before scurrying off.

Lucian places a hand on Dahlia's, rubbing it gently. "Relax, Treasure."

Despite my anxiety, a slight smile plays across my lips. I love the way Lucian calls Dahlia his Treasure. It makes me feel fuzzy inside, but also like I'm intruding on a moment when he looks at her like that.

"I'm trying," Dahlia replies, instantly at ease by her husband's touch.

Their breezy interaction stirs a longing in me.

"I'm sorry," Dahlia says, looking over at me, and I realize I've been staring. Shit, I hope she doesn't think I'm being rude.

"No, no, you're fine," I speak quickly.

"I'm just not used to these things yet, and . . ." she pauses in her thought, glancing at Lucian as if looking for his consent.

He gives her a reassuring nod, lightly squeezing her hand. "You know I don't mind, Treasure."

A relieved smile spreads across Dahlia's face and she squeals to me, "We're four weeks!"

It takes me a moment to understand what she means. Four weeks . . . pregnant!

"Oh, wow," I breathe. "Congratulations!" I can feel her excitement radiating off her.

"Thank you," Dahlia murmurs, shaking her head. "I still can't believe it. I think I checked with the doctor at least five times before finally accepting it as reality."

"It must be an amazing feeling," I say.

"It is," Dahlia agrees. "And I have this guy over here" — she stabs her thumb at Lucian, who chuckles— "to thank for it."

The two exchange a few looks, and I smile, trying to let them have their moment by looking away and sipping the water in my hand while I turn back to the crowd and look for Zander.

I'm about to give up when I spot him near a huge column, talking to his father. A sinking feeling tugs at my stomach as I watch the two men speak to each other. Judging by his father's stiff body language and sharp gestures, I think they're arguing. Although with Zander's expression, maybe not. I feel caught in their exchange.

I wonder what they're fighting over. *Me*, a voice in the back of my head says as I take another nervous sip of my drink. I recognized Dahlia, so I wonder how many men recognize me. And I wouldn't have a clue. They all wear masks in the club. My suspicions are only increased when the man glances my way, a scowl on his face.

For a moment, I feel the urge to jump up and leave, but before I can move, Zander turns from the man and strides toward us. I'm quiet as Lucian says something in Dahlia's ear. I peek up and he has a look of sympathy on his face. *He knows.* I feel sick. I feel Zander next to me before I see him.

"Is everything all right?" I ask Zander as he glides down into the seat next to mine.

Zander gives me a charming smile. "Of course."

He's so smooth with his response that I almost believe him. But I know what I saw.

"So how are things going?" Lucian asks Zander, still holding Dahlia's hand. I watch as his thumb rubs soothing circles on the back of Dahlia's hand.

Their conversation fades into the background as I sit there quietly, my eyes on Dahlia. I can't stop thinking about how happy she looks as she listens to the conversation, a hand on her belly. I bet she'll make a wonderful mother. My throat feels dry as I try to swallow, and I have to bring the glass to my lips and sip the cool water slowly.

"Arianna is an artist," Zander boasts, drawing me out of my thoughts. Lucian looks at me with respect. "Really? That's wonderful."

I blush furiously. "It's nothing really," I downplay. Zander's acting as if I'm an actual painter. I'm not. "It's just a hobby."

"Nonsense," Zander says. "I saw your work. It speaks for itself."

"It's not in any galleries or anything like that," I argue.

"Good enough for me," Zander says firmly.

My cheeks redden even more as Lucian and Dahlia observe our exchange.

"Well that's wonderful," Lucian says, grinning. "I've been thinking about getting a portrait of Dahlia done when she's further along." He glances at his wife, pride in his eyes before looking back at me to say, "Maybe you could do the honor?"

I don't have a moment to respond before Dahlia's eyes widen and she reaches across the small table to grab my hand. "I would love that," she says, and her voice is so full of hope. She looks back at Lucian as though he's just given her a wonderful surprise. "Could you do something like that?" she asks me.

"I haven't done portraits before, but I could." I nod my head slightly although I feel anxious.

Zander reaches behind me and gently massages my back, causing sparks of electricity along wherever he touches. "I'm sure you can," he assures me, his tone encouraging.

I turn to look at him, to thank him, feeling a warmth and relaxation flowing through me, but the moment I do, I freeze.

I didn't know Danny was going to be here.

CHAPTER 19

ZANDER

I can practically feel him the moment he enters. That fucker, Danny Brooks. It's not because of his voice laughing behind me. Or the way Lucian narrows his eyes slightly and pulls Dahlia closer to his side. It's my sweetheart's reaction. Arianna tenses immediately, sucking in a breath between her teeth and straightening her back.

Her eyes lose the brightness that I've only just brought back.

I lean in close to her, ignoring the look from Lucian, and rub the tip of my nose behind her ear. "Relax," I whisper into her ear and gently kiss the tender skin on her upper neck. Her soft hair tickles my nose as I do. I'm a hypocrite for telling her to relax. Nearly a dozen of the men here in this room know I've bought her. They know who she is, and they also know she used to be *his*.

She hasn't noticed the way they've been looking at her. But I have.

Not a single fucker in this room has a clue that Brooks designed this. That he gave her to me to pay his debt, and that this is all a facade. *Unless he's told them.*

I keep the smile plastered on my face as the thought hits me. Bringing the flute to my lips, I take a swig of the sweet champagne, the bubbles tickling the roof of my mouth.

If the men here know that he's given her to me, they're also well aware that I'm letting him pay his debts with her.

And that can't fucking happen.

I hear Brooks laugh again, although it's fainter this time and from across the room through a crowd of people. He should know better than to tell anyone about the arrangement. But he's not a smart man. I put the empty flute to my lips, the glass resting against my bottom lip.

A shiver travels down my arms as Dahlia gently touches Lucian's arm to grab his attention, completely oblivious to the entire situation. Arianna looks away, her head in the opposite direction as Brooks.

I'm struck by the sweet cadence of her voice as a waitress walking by asks for her drink. She politely tells her she's fine as I pass the empty glass to the young woman and she sets it on her silver tray.

"Would you like some fresh air?" Dahlia asks Arianna, and she obediently looks to me before answering.

Lucian speaks up before Arianna can answer, saying, "I could use a moment away from the crowds." His voice is low and only intended for his wife.

"Go ahead," I tell Arianna, nodding my head toward the French doors. She seems a bit more at ease and I think it'd be best if she got the hell out of this room.

"I need to go to the restroom. I'll meet you out there," I answer Arianna and expect her to simply obey. Her hand reaches out to grab my arm as I turn. She's quick to correct herself, shifting slightly with her expression falling and an apology on her lips.

"It's all right," I tell her softly before she can utter a single word, taking her hand in mind and rubbing soothing circles on the back of her knuckles. I stare deep into her dark green eyes, and that's when her reality hits me.

I haven't even considered what she's been through. My stomach churns with a sickness. *What has he done to her?* In a room full of people, all the noises and lights dim to nothing, merely blurs in my periphery as I take in the sadness and fear behind her eyes.

"I've got her," Lucian says, snapping my gaze to his and breaking the small moment of clarity. As he reaches out to her in a casual manner, I nearly rip her away from him, from everyone. In the split second of a moment, I just want to take her away.

I clear my throat, remembering where we are. I straighten my suit and give her a small peck on the cheek. My hand splays across her lower back as I guide her toward Lucian. "I'll be right back, sweetheart."

With a tight smile, she nods her head obediently. Always obeying.

"Don't let her leave your sight," I tell Lucian low enough so only he can hear me. He nods and instinctively glances back toward the crowd, to Brooks.

The smile on my face is nowhere to be seen as I watch him take her away from me, his wife on his right and Arianna on his left.

❄

The sound of running water floods my ears as I wash my hands, staring aimlessly at the lathered suds. The door to the bathroom opens at the same time as a stall door behind me, and it's a reminder that I'm not alone. That I should be performing, but I need to get the fuck out of here.

My eyes finally lift to the mirror, my demeanor not at all what it should be. I can't shake the feeling in the pit of my stomach when I realized she's not okay.

"Payne." The corners of my lips twitch as I hear that bastard's voice. They beg to force my expression into a scowl, but I fight it, concentrating on the fact that a third man is in the room. Stephen Ikabal. He's a clean-cut man with a penchant for younger women. He's been married for three decades, and I highly doubt he's been faithful for any of those years. But then again, she hasn't been either. They both prefer younger company, or so I've heard.

"Brooks," I say and finally tear my eyes away from

Stephen in the mirror as he washes his hands in the basin two down from mine.

"How are you?" Brooks cocks an eyebrow, leaning against the granite counter and facing me. Stephen doesn't react, but he's a coy old man. I'm sure he's listening. Everyone's always listening. Always watching for a weakness. When you're on top, it's so easy to fall.

I force a charming smile onto my face as I dry my hands, my eyes on Brooks. He fooled me. I had no idea gambling was his vice. I thought it was sadism. The thought chills my blood and for a moment, the charm, dimples and all, slips as I think about my sweetheart. It doesn't make sense how they fit. It just doesn't add up.

"Well, and you?" I answer him. Although I'm relaxed and engaging Brooks, I'm highly aware of Stephen's presence as he turns off the faucet and dries his own hands. I need him to get the fuck out of here. I want nothing more than to grab this asshole by the collar and shove him against the wall. I need to know what he's done to her to put that fear in her eyes.

Brooks nods his head, a smile on his face that looks cocky as his eyes flicker to Stephen as he passes us to get to the door. "Just missing my Arianna a bit." His voice is chipper as he shrugs his shoulders. Every hair stands on end as Stephen pauses by the trashcan before tossing in the balled-up paper towel.

A chill sweeps across every inch of my skin. I can only imagine what they think of her if he's been running his mouth. And I fucking hate it.

"I hope you're getting your money's worth," Brooks says

beneath his breath, but loud enough for Stephen to hear on his way out. The creak of the door opening and then falling closed easily is the only noise in the room as my hand balls into a fist, the skin tightening around my knuckles to the point where I'm convinced it will split.

I don't wait for the door to close all the way. I don't even lock it like I know I should. I can't hold back the rage any longer.

I hit his jaw first, taking him by surprise. Maybe he expected me to act the part in this environment. After all, we're not alone in his office. The soft classical music spills through the bottom of the door as I grip his collar and hit him again with my right fist, knocking his head backward.

This time, he expects it at least and he hits me back square on the nose, the pain radiating outward up my cheeks and to the back of my head. It nearly makes me lose my grip on him, but I hold on. White noise rings in my ears as I quickly push him backward.

"She's not yours anymore," I sneer into his face as my hands clench, and I slam his back against the tiled wall. I hear a crack, but it does nothing to stop me. "You gave her to me, remember?"

My teeth slam against one another so hard that I swear they'll crack. He merely grins back at me, blood coating his teeth on the right side of his crooked smile.

As I talk, I can feel warm blood trickle from under my nose. My instant reaction is to slam him back against the wall, and I do it just to get the aggression out. "You owe me, and you'll pay me by the twenty-fifth." I decide then that even if I can't convince her not to give him the money, I won't accept it. I'll wait to pay her. I'll refuse to do it until after Brooks has paid me.

"Sure," he says with a glint in his eyes.

"I won't be paying Arianna, so you'll need to come up with that money some other way," I say without thinking, holding his gaze and watching the arrogant expression morph into fear. It doesn't matter if or when I transfer the money to Arianna. I won't let him steal from her. I won't let him use her. Not anymore.

I let go of him when the fear is so strong that his body is stiff. I glance at myself in the mirror and see a black eye already forming, blood on my face and also my dress shirt. *Fuck!*

"And then what? What are you really going to do about it?" he asks as I grab a few paper towels and wipe the blood from under my nose. He doesn't move off the wall as he hisses, "I don't have the fucking money."

I don't answer him. I won't ever say it out loud. *I'll kill him.* Not for the debt, but for what he's done to her.

"We had a deal." He pushes the words through clenched teeth. "You have her and you can't go back on that!"

It hits me then what I've done. How I've lost control. I've provided evidence. Security cameras are littered in this building. Fuck!

"Payne?" Brooks calls out to me, but I ignore him. He means for it to come out strong as he stays behind me, standing tall and putting on a front, but his voice cracks with fear.

Tossing the paper towel into the trash, I open the door and almost make a quick right turn. I hesitate in the doorway. I need to get the fuck out of here. I can't be seen like this. But I need to get Arianna. The sound of another man coming down the small hallway makes me move. I have five minutes. If I don't have her in my grasp in five minutes, I'm coming back.

I keep my hand up, my fingers pinching the bridge of my nose and covering my face. To any onlookers, I hope it looks as if I have a headache. The cool air from the outside breezes by me as I get closer to the exit and a couple walks in.

I ignore them. I can't even see who they are and I don't give a fuck.

As soon as I get outside, I spot my limo and walk straight to it. I keep my strides wide and my pace fast. It's on the far left of the parking lot and the valet and a few guests are on my right, the sounds of them chatting and the brighter lights of the entrance dimming as I walk farther into the darkened lot.

I notice Marcus look up and see me, a surprised look on his face as I finally lower my hand and wipe under my nose. Dark red blood smears across the arm of my jacket.

That fucker. My steps are hard as I stalk toward the limo, my blood fueled with the desire to go back. I clench and unclench my hands before reaching for my phone. *My sweetheart.*

Thank fuck for Lucian.

As Marcus opens the door, not daring to look me in the eyes, I slip the phone from my pocket, only then realizing my knuckles are cracked and there's blood on them, too.

My blood runs cold as I settle into the seat. The door closes shut with a loud click and silences the cabin of the limo as I dial his number.

"Lucian," I say and press the phone close to my ear as I stare at the entrance, the light from the large glass doors and windows spilling out into the night.

"Zander?" he says, and his voice is filled with surprise. Which is a good thing. It calms my racing heart.

"Arianna's still with you?" I ask as the driver's door opens and Marcus slips in. His eyes flash to mine for a moment in the rearview mirror.

"She is. Is everything—"

"Bring her to the front . . . please," I ask him quickly, grabbing a few tissues from the side compartment as I feel a bit of blood trickle from my nose. I resist the urge to slam my fist against the door. Against anything. The anger is coming back. I shouldn't have left him like that. *He deserves so much worse.*

"Of course," Lucian is quick to agree, a serious note in his tone.

"Thank you." I barely get the words out, feeling in that moment that I've failed her.

Every muscle in me is wound tight, my heart beating

chaotically. I've never done something so fucking stupid before in my life.

"To the entrance, Sir?" Marcus asks, and I clench my jaw, nodding my head as his eyes meet mine again in the rearview mirror. My heart slows, and I reach for the whiskey as the limo pulls out slowly. I grab the glass and ice out of habit and pour two fingers into the glass. I sway slightly as we drive around to the front.

I'm able to down the glass before he stops the car and gets out, the cold ice clashing against my teeth. I don't even realize she's waiting for us until Marcus gets out and opens her door.

I run a hand down my face and put the cup back as she climbs in, her dress bunched in her hands.

My chest feels tight and my heart clenches as I watch her step carefully in and settle next to me. I've made a fool of myself. And her. All because of Brooks.

Next time, she doesn't leave my side. Not for a moment.

"I'm sorry." I choke the words out, reaching for her with my left hand, the one without the torn knuckles as Marcus closes the door. I'm so fucking ashamed. She deserves better than this.

She shakes her head easily, her brows pinched and her mouth parting as she takes in the sight of me. "Zander," she says, and my name is barely a whisper on her lips.

She reaches up in an attempt to touch my face. From the look in her eyes, it must be bad. They're full of questions. But she doesn't ask them. She already knows the answers. I snatch her hand in mine before she can touch me.

"Don't," I tell her. At first, hurt flashes in her eyes, but I'm quick to add, "Just . . ." I trail off and take in a long inhale, not knowing what to say or what to tell her. But I don't have to. She lies down, not waiting for me to finish as the limo pulls ahead. Her hair spills over my leg as she rests her head in my lap, laying her cheek against the designer pants.

I slowly pet her hair, moving it from her face and smoothing it out. She lets out a comfortable sigh. As she nestles her head into my lap, looking aimlessly into the cabin of the limo, her small hand wraps around my knee. Her thumb rubs small circles. "Was it Danny?" she asks me.

"Yes," I answer her easily.

"Are you okay?" she asks me in a cautious breath.

"Fine," I reply, and I'm short with her, my voice hard as I continue. "You'll never go back to him." Her finger halts in its rhythmic path as I say the words with authority, as if I can command her. For now, she may be in a contract, but I'm not a fool. I can't force her after the thirty days are done. She doesn't owe me a damn thing, and what's more is that I don't want to force her.

She doesn't answer me, and her body is stiff, but I continue to pet her hair and then run my fingers down her shoulder to the dip of her waist and back up.

"I don't want you to."

Her cheek rubs against my leg as she nods her head, but she still doesn't answer me.

She has no idea what I feel for her. She may think she's still just a pawn and a bargaining chip.

But I'll be damned if she ever sees that asshole again.

I'm never letting her go.

CHAPTER 20

ARIANNA

"You should really let me take a look at your eye," I say to Zander once we step inside his estate and make our way to his bedroom. I'm following behind him, not even taking in his house as he leads me up the stairs.

My heart is still reeling, twisting in my chest with a mix of emotions, my mind running with a million questions.

I don't know what Danny did to him, but I feel caught in the middle. I feel like I'm the one to blame. He was there because of me. Had to be. Now Zander is paying for it.

Zander doesn't answer me as he pushes open his bedroom door and walks over to the mirror to peer at his face. Even roughed up, he looks sexy as fuck, his bloodstained dress shirt torn open at the front, his hard, tanned flesh on display.

"I'm fine," he mutters. But it's not reflected in his voice.

"Well let me——," I start to say, coming up behind him.

"I'm good," Zander cuts in. My forehead's pinched, and I'm silent for a moment as he takes off his suit jacket, tossing it to the side and then removes his ruined dress shirt, tugging it over his head. He takes it off and lets it drop to the floor, seemingly ignoring my presence.

I can't help my frown and need to back away from him, feeling slightly dejected. He's blowing me off when I want to know what happened. I let out a heavy but silent breath of frustration as my gaze drops to the floor and I chew on my bottom lip. I wish he'd just talk to me. I need to know what's going on. I feel guilty, like Zander's bruised face is all my fault. And this is only making me feel worse.

"Hey," Zander says, getting my attention before he lifts my chin up so my eyes meet his. "It's okay." He says the words with conviction, and I almost believe it. "I promise you."

I nod my head slightly and my voice cracks as I answer him. "Okay."

"I'm still pissed. At Danny, and at myself." He drops his hand as he adds, "But I promise you that everything is all right." His eyes search mine, and I finally let his words sink in. I believe him. I trust him.

"I'm just glad you're okay," I say quietly.

"I'll always be okay," Zander replies with confidence, his hand cupping my cheek again. "It's you I'm worried about."

"Me?" I ask.

Zander nods, gently stroking the side of my face. My skin warms with his gentle strokes, my pulse quickening.

"I'm fine," I answer him. "Really, I'm fine." His eyes search mine for a long moment.

"You've been denied so much. I want to give you . . . more."

His words leave me with a pain in my heart that I don't quite understand, and I feel as if I'm in a trance staring into his eyes. I wish I had words, but I don't. I step closer to him, just wanting to feel him. All I know is that I need his touch.

"You looked so beautiful tonight," he says softly.

A flush comes to my cheeks as I breathe, "Thank you."

"And I've been waiting all night for this." He kisses me, pressing his lips softly against mine. It's sweet and short, but it leaves me wanting more when he pulls away.

"I need you," he says, his voice low and heavy.

I don't even think about the words as they leave me. "Take me," I moan, my heart pounding in my chest, hungry for more.

Zander spears his fingers through my hair, cradling the back of my head, and gives me a deeper kiss, this one filled with swirling tongue and unbridled passion. I melt into his hard body, feeling weak in the knees, but he holds me up with his powerful arms.

I moan into his mouth, fire heating my core, my skin blazing from the heat of his hard body. He sucks on my tongue in response, pulling me closer to him. Down below, I can feel his hardening cock against my stomach.

He breaks away from our kiss, his lips finding my neck, his hands sliding down my back to cup my ass. I moan, throwing my head back, his lips burning into my flesh.

"Fuck," he groans, his lips near my ears as he smothers my neck with passionate kisses. "I want that sweet, tight pussy on my cock." I go limp in his arms, weak from his passion, and he picks me up, carrying me to the bed.

He lays me down gently, his breathing ragged, his eyes on my face and shining with lust as he climbs into the bed, making it creak as he places his hands to either side of my head.

"You're so fucking beautiful," he tells me, his voice low and hoarse, his breath hot on my face.

"I want you, too," I answer him quickly. I do. I've never wanted something so much.

Zander's lips find my neck again, pecking, kissing, licking, causing me to throw my head back, my nipples pebbling and my body burning up in flames.

He makes his way down my neck, pausing briefly to pull my gown above my shoulders and toss it carelessly onto the bedroom floor. Next comes my bra, Zander practically tearing it off and slinging it across the room. His eyes immediately feast on my hard nipples, his chest heaving as he moves in and takes a nipple into his mouth. He swirls his tongue around it at first, teasing, tweaking it, before sucking on it with great force as my back arches in response.

I buck slightly at the sensation, biting down on my lip as I grab onto the bedding. He gives both nipples equal attention, alternating from one to another before moving down my stomach, his lips kissing every inch of my sensitive skin along the way.

When he reaches my hips, he grabs my panties and pulls them off, baring my glistening sex to him. Below, I hear him inhale deeply and bury his face between my legs before taking a languid lick of my pussy.

"Oh," I moan as his tongue flicks back and forth against my clit.

I try to keep still as he tastes me and sucks my clit, pleasure stirring in my belly. But before I reach my peak, he moves in closer, causing the bed to creak as he hoists both of my legs around his shoulders, burying his face into my pussy, clamping his mouth down on my clit as hard as he can.

"Oh, God!" I yell as he has his way with me, savagely tasting me and sucking on my clit until the pleasure is too much.

A fire builds in my core as he goes to town on me, and I grip the bedding with both hands, digging my nails into the plush comforter. His keen blue eyes look up at me but it's so hard to look back, my neck wanting to arch away, my body begging me for both an escape but also for more.

Keeping his eyes locked with mine, Zander plunges two thick fingers into my pussy while keeping his mouth clamped down on my clit with great force.

His forceful touch, his relentless sucking and intense gaze are all I can handle, the fiery storm exploding with fury from my core, ripping through my body like a level six tornado.

"Fuck!" I scream as explosions of insane pleasure rock my body. All the while, Zander keeps me in place, his eyes locked on my face, his mouth clamped on my pussy as my limbs convulse violently from orgasm after orgasm. "Zander!"

I don't know when he lets me go. I'm so overwhelmed with ecstasy, but suddenly, he's stripping in front of me, pulling off his pants and underwear, letting his cock spring free as he tosses his clothes onto the floor.

"Now it's my turn," he growls hungrily, lining his thick cock up between my legs and thrusting inside me without hesitation.

I gasp as he enters me, feeling him fill me, stretching my walls, while he groans with utter rapture.

"Fuck," he says, his deep voice low and heavy, "You're so fucking tight."

He places his hands to either side of me to balance himself, getting into position to pound harder into me while my hands instinctively drift down to his chiseled ass, my fingernails digging into his flesh.

His breathing is ragged as he steadies himself, all the while keeping up his ruthless pace. When he gets his balance, he fucks me harder and deeper, rocking the bed back and forth, the headboard starting to bang against the wall.

The smack of flesh hitting flesh fills the room, mixing in with the sounds of the banging headboard. *Smack. Smack. Smack. Bang. Bang. Bang.* I can't scream. I want to scream out my pleasure, but my body feels paralyzed from the intensity of it all. I feel another storm brewing as I moan out his name in what feels like a whispered plea, barely able to take his entire length, his cock going so deeply I almost think it's too much.

Zander picks up his pace, his chiseled hips thrusting violently inward, faster, harder, his moaning becoming louder as I feel his cock grow impossibly hard inside me. It's coming. I know it. And I want it. *All of it.*

His powerful thrusts slow down to deep, rhythmic ones, the bed indenting each time his body smashes into me with such force that I fear the box spring might break.

"Fuck, I'm gonna cum," I hear Zander moan while the fire inside my core ignites again.

One. Two. Three. Four. Each thrust is deeper and harder than before, and on the fourth, Zander throws back his head as he goes balls deep inside me and cums violently.

My thighs are quivering and shaking like an earthquake as a tidal wave of pleasure hits me and I moan his name over and over.

"Zander!" I cry, feeling his dick still contracting inside me while my walls squeeze every last drop out of him.

Finally, he pulls out of me and falls onto the bed on my right side, his chest heaving from exertion, his body covered in sweat. Both of us need to catch our breath.

As he walks away from me, I'm struck by the realization

that my body is shaking with an intensity I've never felt before. Every emotion feels as if it's overwhelming me.

I've had sex before. I've had other partners and come before.

But this is different.

It's so strong, so powerful. It's . . . too intense. I place a hand over my racing heart as he flicks on the light to the bathroom.

The shockwaves pulse through me as I try to calm down and try to ignore what my heart is telling me.

CHAPTER 21

ZANDER

My light blue gaze stares back at me in the mirror of the dresser. A dark ring is around my left eye. This isn't a good look. My eyes travel to Arianna's form on the bed behind me as I slip the Rolex around my wrist and tighten the band. I don't even need to look as I do it. It's been the same every morning. But there's never been a woman behind me.

In my room, on my bed.

Her gorgeous body is nothing but a small lump on the bed, hidden beneath the thick grey comforter. She's getting to me. I'm breaking rules for her. A deep inhale makes my back crack slightly as I close my eyes, wincing slightly from the bruise on my face. Last night . . . things are changing. Fast. And it's hard to admit it.

I got into a fucking bathroom brawl over her. *It was worth it.*

Work is calling me. I'm already late. I button the top of

my dress shirt, not knowing what to do about my sweetheart.

Right now . . . and later. Once all of this is done. I'm sure as fuck not kicking her out, but I don't like that she'll be in here. Alone.

With cold blood running through my veins, I quietly walk to the end of the bed, my jacket and shoes waiting for me.

The clock on the nightstand reads 6:40. Late for me, but Arianna's still asleep. A genuine smile curves my lips up when I hear her soft snoring. It's adorable. *She's* adorable.

With her mouth parted slightly, the soft sound is accompanied by the slight rise of her shoulders, her dark hair a messy halo around her angelic face.

She's so beautiful. So innocent.

I rip my gaze away, slipping the first shoe on and tying the laces tight.

My daily routine. Nothing has changed. I almost roll my eyes at the thought, pulling the laces even tighter.

Everything's changed.

It's not because of Arianna. I refuse to think that she's the reason I'm slipping, making one mistake after the other. It's Danny Brooks. I keep making errors in my judgment when it comes to him.

The thin laces dig into my fingers as I tie the second shoe and rise from the bench at the end of the bed, picking up my coat and walking quietly to the nightstand where I tossed my keys last night.

I have to close my eyes when I catch her sweet scent. It's like citrus with a hint of honeysuckle. I wonder if she knows how alluring she is. Lying there so beautifully, her body so soft and warm with curves that only tempt me that much more.

A dark voice in the back of my head whispers in nearly a hiss.

You can take her. She's yours. You own her.

But the stolen moments we've had are because she wanted me. Because she needed me.

I don't want her to think I'm the kind of partner Brooks was. The thought disgusts me. My nose wrinkles and I turn sharply away from her, hating the vile image of that prick. If that's what last night was for her, I'll never forgive myself. She's not a whore for me to use. Not to me. My heart beats faster, slamming against my chest.

The keys jingle against one another as I snatch them quickly off the dresser. I can be a Master worthy of her. Not a sick fuck who uses pain as a threat. I don't ever want to cause her pain, and I know she doesn't need it. Even if she thinks she does. Holding the car keys in my hand, I walk away from her, intent on leaving both her and my thoughts behind me.

I'm halfway across the room when her soft voice calls out. "Zander?" My name is soft, but also scratchy, the morning evident in her tone.

I stop in my tracks, the floorboards beneath the thick

carpet creaking slightly. My body tenses, realizing I have to address her now. She knows I heard her.

I turn slightly, relaxing my body and treating her the same way I treat everyone else. With a facade of ease. It comes naturally.

"Good morning," I greet her and feel the fake smile on my face without consenting to it.

She props her small body up on her elbow and shoves the hair away from her face. Blinking several times, each time seeming more and more awake, she stifles a yawn and rises slowly into a sitting position, gripping the comforter in her hands and bringing it up over her naked body. I'm not sure if it's because she's self-conscious or if she doesn't want me seeing her.

In the soft yellow morning light spilling between the thick curtains, she looks radiant. I *want* to see her, every last inch of her, just like I did last night. *But it's only fair that she hides herself behind a blanket while I hide behind this smile.*

Her dark green eyes dart to the bedroom door and then back to me as she asks, "Do you want me to get ready?" Another yawn creeps up on her, and from the look in her eyes, she's obviously embarrassed by her exhaustion.

"You don't have to," I say, and my voice is strong, perhaps slightly harsh.

"Are you sure?" she asks me sweetly. "I don't mind . . . I know you probably don't want me in here . . ." Her voice trails off as she picks at the comforter and then laughs a little, this sweet little sound that's so pure.

My smile softens and I'm moving toward her before I even realize it, my strides easy and comfortable. I have the urge to sit on the bed. She even scoots slightly, making room and straightening a little, although the comforter sags slightly in front of her. Just a glimpse of her cleavage is showing, modest but tempting. Just like my sweetheart.

I almost sit with her, but then I remember. *Her gift.*

It was meant to be a thank you for attending last night.

"I got you something," I tell her without thinking. Instantly, her expression softens. Those sweet lips slowly turn up and her eyes sparkle. I run my hand through my hair, wondering if it's stupid. All the while, I'm going to the closet and gathering the small bag to give to my sweetheart. Her eyes flicker to the empty side of the bed, a warm red hue filling her cheeks. My spot that she made for me.

Utterly gorgeous. A huff of air leaves me as I look at her. She really doesn't get how tempting she is. How a woman like her could ruin a man like me. Losing control, coming undone all because of her. It's already happening. And she doesn't even know it. My feet remain planted where they are, even though my body wills me to sit next to her. I have to hold back.

I clear my throat as I hold the bag out to her. At the faint sound, Arianna finally looks at me. I watch her face as her slender fingers pull the paper away.

The thick wrapping paper crinkles as she pulls the package out of the bag and tears it open from the seams.

The moment she realizes what they are, her eyes brighten and a wide smile makes my chest fill with confidence. She's so true to her feelings, her reactions so natural.

And she loves the gift.

"Brushes?" she asks me with that smile still on her face. Her eyes aren't on me though. She's peeling the last bit of tape from the package of paintbrushes. I had no idea such a thing could cost so much.

"I thought you'd like them," I answer her simply.

She tilts her head, focusing all of her attention on me as she puts it all to the side and rises to her knees, pulling the comforter with her and planting a small, chaste kiss on my lips.

My eyes stay open the entire time, and although her lips are pursed, I swear she doesn't stop smiling. She pulls back quickly, that beautiful red flush all over her skin, and says softly, "Thank you. I love them."

I stare at her a long moment, realizing how genuinely happy she is with such a small gift. But the clock from the nightstand calls my attention with the faint click of the hand.

Late. I'm late.

Reality sets in, and I give her a nod. "I'm happy you like them. I've got to be going now."

An awkward tension settles between us.

"Do you want me to go?" she asks, the warm color

fading and a wall of armor slowly rising around her. The small moment is over, enjoyable though it was.

"No," I say, but even I can hear the hesitation in my voice. I strengthen it as I add, "You can stay for as long as you'd like."

I lean forward, my legs pushing against the bed making it groan and a hand bracing myself on the bed. I cup her jaw with my other hand to kiss her quickly, pulling back slightly and staring at her lips for just a moment. She doesn't open her eyes until I let her go.

CHAPTER 22

ARIANNA

I run my fingers over the paintbrushes, my gift from Zander. They're the most beautiful brushes I've ever seen, with high-quality mahogany handles, exquisite markings, and fine, durable bristles. I press them to my chest, a fuzzy feeling swirling in the pit of my stomach. I feel like a stupid little girl, but I don't care. It's nice to be given something that means so much. Even if it didn't mean much to him.

These are even better than the gown Zander gifted me. And I can see myself putting them to good use, already thinking about the masterpieces I'll paint. I'll cherish them long after this contract is over.

When this is *over*.

The thought makes me sick to my stomach. I'm getting used to Zander and his charming personality, and I feel like I'm just starting to get to know him.

But do you really know him? says that annoying voice in the back of my head. *This is all supposed to be fake, a make-*

believe courtship. You can't really know a man who is hiding behind a facade.

I chew my lower lip, dropping the brushes into my lap.

I don't want to believe that everything Zander says or does is inauthentic. When he looks at me, fire burning in his eyes, it looks real. Each time I'm with him, I can *feel* the emotion emanating from him. I *feel* the connection we have between each other. It can't be fake, can it? Why would he ask me to stay as long as I like if it were make-believe?

Because he wants you to believe it's real.

I don't know what to believe at this point. I feel so many conflicting emotions. I want Zander. And I want him to truly want me, too. But I know less about him than I do about Danny. And that doesn't sit well with me.

The voice resurfaces with, *Well, you have the whole house to yourself. Why don't you find out?*

For once, I agree with the voice. I set the brushes aside and roll out of bed, my feet causing the floor to creak as I slip on one of his shirts and walk out of the bedroom and into the hall.

I take a tour of the house, going room from room, looking around for anything untoward and taken in by the opulence. I'm really impressed with the house, every room filled with expensive furniture and superbly decorated. It's large, luxurious, and beautiful. But after a while, it starts to feel empty. There are too many rooms for just one man. Zander has to be lonely living here.

But he has me now.

I huff out a chuckle at my wishful thinking as I run my hand over a painted glass vase in one of the extra bedrooms. I bet it costs more than what I make in a month. For how long will he have me? A month? Two? I shake my head. It might be not much longer than that.

I make my way back into the hallway, my bare feet padding along the gleaming hardwood floors. I try to get rid of the overwhelming feeling that I don't belong here, but with each step, the gnawing feeling in the pit of my stomach grows and grows. I'm about to turn around and go back to the room to grab the gown and my purse to get out of here when I see a picture frame on a small, dark stand near the entryway to one of the common areas of the house.

I pick it up out of instinct. It doesn't belong here either. I already know it. While everything else in Zander's house is expensive and each item holds an air of luxury, this picture frame is common. And the photo inside it, just a snapshot.

It's an old family picture with Zander, maybe ten years old, with his father and a lady whom I presume to be his mother. She's a beautiful woman, with long, flowing blonde hair and a shapely figure. I can definitely see where Zander got some of his looks from.

But what attracts me most to her is the way she looks at Zander. It's the way all mothers look at their children. A heavy feeling settles on my chest as I stare at his mother's face.

It takes me a moment to realize that I've met Zander's father but not his mother. I find it odd that he's never mentioned her before at all. The idea hits me that I should Google Zander's family. I bet there's at least some dirt on his father . . . maybe some on Zander, too.

I'm so dumb. I should've done this the moment I found out about Zander.

I'm quick to go back to the bedroom and take out my cell. I bring up the web browser, tapping in *Zander Payne*. The first few results yield nothing. I go several pages without seeing anything actually related to Zander or his family. It's all business news. I let out a sigh of relief when I don't really find anything. At least Zander doesn't have a sinister past.

I'm about to search for something more specific when one headline grabs my attention

Rich Socialite takes her own life after husband's affair.

Marie Payne, forty-eight-year-old wife of wealthy hedge fund investor Thomas Payne, jumped to her death after learning of her husband's years-long affair with his mistress. Sources say in the week leading up to her death, Marie was so distraught she locked herself away in her room for days at a time, refusing to come out for food or drink.

Marie leaves behind a young son, Zander Payne . . .

"Oh," I breathe, tearing my eyes away from the article, tears filling my eyes. My body seems to go cold all at once, the large bed feeling like an abyss as I bring the comforter up and around me. I check the date on the article and think back to how old Zander was.

He was just a boy. I wipe under my eyes as the sting of the tears hits me out of nowhere.

No wonder he keeps secrets, I say to myself, shaking my head and holding my tears at bay. *No wonder Zander doesn't trust people.*

I thought I had a painful life, but at least I'm still alive. A lot of my issues, I caused myself. Being a problem child, being wild and partying. But his mother's death? Zander had no control over that. No control over the betrayal that led to such an earth-shattering loss.

Letting out a deep, trembling sigh, I turn my phone off and settle into the comforter, imagining how hard that had to be on him. I'm no longer in the mood to go snooping around. After finding that out, a part of me is content in letting Zander keep whatever secrets he has close to his chest. It probably gives him comfort, more control over his life. And who am I to say that he owes me complete access?

I look toward the door to his bedroom, feeling a swell of emotion. I need a release. I need to do something that'll make me feel better.

There's only one thing that I know will do that.

I throw the covers off me and go back through his house, looking for his office. After finding pen and paper, I make my way to the piano room, sprawling out on the floor.

CHAPTER 23

ZANDER

My hand tightens on the leather shifter as I park my Mercedes in the garage. I lean back in my seat after turning the keys and pulling them out. My forehead is pinched as I stare at the garage door to my home.

She's still inside.

I didn't expect it. There are monitors and cameras set up throughout my home. I'd be a fucking idiot not to have them with the sheer number of people who come in and out. From the housekeeping service, to caterers and business associates.

I wasn't surprised when she started looking through my things. I rest my head back against the leather, staring at the door and remembering how I watched her on the computer screen rather than actually working today. I'd already decided phone conferences would have to substitute for my normal meetings, considering the faint darkness under my left eye. I canceled three of them, though, so I could focus on watching her. During the fourth and fifth, she stayed on my screen, lying on the floor, sprawled out and tempting me to come back to her. To pull her tempting body into mine, but also to see her drawing.

My sweetheart is a beautiful distraction.

And she's still here.

Or at least she was when I left the office nearly fifteen minutes ago. The realization that she could be done with her art makes me exit the car in haste. Shoving the keys into my pocket, I open the door and kick it shut behind me. The garage is at the side of the house, and I'm well aware that my pace is much faster than it usually is. I'm curious to see if she's still sprawled there on the floor of the piano room, waiting for me.

My dick hardens in my pants as the mental images of me lying on the ground next to her and slowly teasing her shoulder with my fingertips until she shivers plays in my mind. But when I get to the foyer and see her spot empty, my steps slow and my heart pauses in my chest. She's been here for hours. Taunting me to come home.

I stare at the gleaming hardwood floor. How the fuck have I missed her? How cruel would it be for her to leave just as I've come home when I've been wanting her all day? The seconds split and time moves slower as anger seeps in. *She's mine.* She should be here. Waiting for me.

I know it's unreasonable. Even as my jaw clenches, I know I shouldn't think that way. This is *pretend*. It's fake and merely a result of my poor judgment, but nonetheless, *I want her*. And she was fucking here all this time.

"Oh!" the small sound of her gasp from behind me grips my attention. I school my expression, turning slowly to see her standing in the kitchen. I haven't missed her. The adrenaline stops pumping in my blood. My heartbeat settles and my body instantly relaxes at the sight of her in the middle of the kitchen. My sweetheart didn't slip through my fingers. She's right where she belongs.

Her dark green eyes are wide and she shuffles her feet as she stares back at me. She pulls her hair around her shoulder, her fingers nervously twirling the ends. "I wasn't sure . . ." she starts to say something but stops as I walk toward her in the open kitchen, my strides slow and deliberate.

"I'm surprised you're still here," I say, and the lie comes out with an unnatural tone in my voice that I don't recognize.

Arianna doesn't notice as she clasps her hands and shakes her head. "I'm sorry. I didn't have work today, and I got caught up." Her hands fly outward as she blurts out an excuse, and the paper she's been working on waves in the air as she moves her hands.

"What's that?" I ask her, nodding to the sketch. I resist the urge to take the few remaining steps forward and snatch it from her. I want her to *want* to show me.

"Oh," she says and looks at the paper as if it's the first time she's seen it. As if it didn't encompass the last few hours of her time.

"May I see?" I ask, but the words come out as a hard command instead of a question and I wish I could stop them. I wish I could soften for her. But that's not who I am. "Please," I add and clear my throat.

She doesn't react to the harsh tone. Instead, she obediently hands me the paper, and the thrill of her listening to me makes my blood heat with desire. Such a small thing. So insignificant really. But she makes me feel powerful in a way I haven't felt before. She makes me want to command her. It's a dangerous thing for her to play with me like this, to tempt me, but she doesn't realize she's doing it.

She bites down on her bottom lip as I take the paper from her. I'm gentle with the edges, and I make sure not to touch any of the marks. Her eyes watch where I touch the paper, and her fingertips are covered in ink of some sort. I shake the paper slightly, finally getting to see what she's been working on all this time.

And it's beautiful. I knew she wouldn't disappoint me.

It's just a sketch of the room. Of the piano, really. But the way it's done romanticizes the barren room. Something about the subtlety of the lines, the delicate details and shading. There's a softness to it that I've never felt in that room myself. But it's what she sees. What she *feels* being there. It makes me see it in a different light.

"You have such talent, sweetheart." I lift my eyes from the sketch to her eyes and love how much light shines back at me.

"Thank you," she says in a whisper, a blush coloring her chest and moving up to her cheeks.

"You should do this . . . for a living." Her long lashes whip up as she stares back at me. "It's a crime that you do anything other than this."

I expect a smile in return, but instead, she answers kindly but firmly, "I can't. I have work, and . . . I just can't."

"I'll get you a studio tomorrow," I say out loud without thinking. It was a fleeting thought in my office, but hearing her now, I know I need to get her one.

"A studio?" she asks me with disbelief.

I nod my head, my brow furrowing as I second-guess what it's called. "For your art," I state and gesture to the paper in her hand.

There's still a look of confusion on her face. Her soft lips part, but no words come out. She clears her throat, looking away from me.

"What's wrong?" I ask her, taking another step closer but standing an arm's length away. The warmth from this morning is gone. The girl I held in my arms last night isn't the same one standing in front of me.

"It just seems . . . a bit much?" she responds after a moment.

I can tell she's trying to distance herself. She's already waiting for this contract to be over, perhaps so she can stop playing the part. So she can just go back to being herself. *To being Brooks's possession to barter off when he sees fit.* The second the thought comes to my mind, jealousy ravages my thoughts.

And for the first time in years, I show it. My expression, my stance, everything shows what I'm feeling and thinking. I can't stop it. Arianna takes a small step back, fear clearly evident as she reacts to my anger.

I shake my head slightly, letting out a heavy exhale and pinching the bridge of my nose, hating that I've scared her. I don't want to hide anymore, but my anger isn't for her. None of it. But this is why I hide it.

"You're playing the part of my girlfriend." I start speaking without thinking, convincing both of us that a studio is necessary for this . . . game. "They'll expect me to pamper you." I finally open my eyes and chance a look at her. "I would do anything for someone I want to impress." *For you*, that dark voice in my head whispers. *For someone I want to love me.*

I ignore the thought, a chill traveling down my spine as Arianna slowly nods her head. She visibly swallows, still a bit unsure of herself.

But she answers with the words I want to hear. "Okay," she says, and her voice is soft, meant to appease me. "Thank you."

My eyes search hers, but she isn't looking at me. I chance a step toward her and cup her jaw like I did this morning. Her posture softens and she pushes her cheek against my palm, her small hand cupping the back of mine and her eyes shining back at me with vulnerability. "Let me spoil you, sweetheart," I speak slowly. "Just for the rest of the contract."

I've told many lies in my life. So many deceitful things

have left my lips. And I know full well the words that just slipped past my lips are nothing but a deception.

I said them only to get her to cave to me. I want her to submit to me. I can feel that darkness in me rising. A possessive side is controlling me. And I don't stop it. I don't even want to suppress it.

She's making me weak. And for the first time in my life, I don't give a fuck.

CHAPTER 24

ARIANNA

Let me spoil you, sweetheart.

Zander's words run through my mind, causing warmth to flow through my chest. I told him yes, only for the contract. *But that was a lie.* I want to get lost in his world and become his plaything. I want to fulfill his every desire, all while being spoiled by him. It's a fantasy and it's dangerous to get lost in it, but I am. I'm becoming consumed with the thought of being *his* and losing sight on what the reality of this situation is.

Each day that passes, I feel more at ease, wanting more and more of what he has to offer.

I suck in a deep breath as I gaze out the floor-to-ceiling windows, remembering the way he looked at me the other day. There was something in his eyes. Something that told me what we have feels real. I want to believe it. But it's too good to be true. And like most things that are too good to be true, it's easy to be fooled. I don't want to be that girl, hoping and wishing for something that can never be, all while ignoring the truth. Everyone knows that in real life, there are no Prince Charmings and no knights in shining armor. Still, I'm drawn to him like a moth to a flame.

"There you are," says Zander's deep voice behind me.

I turn around with my eyes closed, wanting to believe in the fantasy. And when I open them, I'm lost in the world I want. In the make-believe. He's leaning against the doorjamb in the doorway, wearing dress pants and a matching dress shirt, looking classically handsome and sexy as fuck. My breath halts in my lungs, refusing to leave the moment. This is real. If only I could hold onto it.

"Here I am," I say, flashing a light smile, ignoring my racing heart, the fear, and every other thing that's going to rip us apart and leave me shredded into nothingness. I can pretend. For him.

Zander grins at me, walking over to deliver a warm kiss on my lips. I like this smile. There's something different about it than the way he smiles at everyone else. This one is just for me. I think it's the way his eyes brighten and the skin around them wrinkles. I nearly melt into his hard body, my knees going weak from *that* look.

When he pulls away, I'm breathless and feeling drunk on lust. If he wanted to take me right here, right now, I wouldn't dare object.

"Are you ready to go see the studio?" he asks me, gently rubbing my arm and causing sparks to flow through my body.

I gaze up into his eyes, seeing the caring warmth reflected there.

All the questions are right there, on the tip of my tongue. Is he going to keep me afterward? Does this feel the same to him? I'm falling into a dark abyss and I'm terrified. I just want to know that he'll catch me. But closing my eyes and imagining he will makes the fall that much easier, that much more enjoyable. Even if there's nothing but the hard, cold, unforgiving ground there to meet me when this is all over.

His eyes stare back at me as the questions makes my stomach flutter, but my lips stay closed tight. My heart is clenching in agony because I already know the answers. I already know the truth.

And I refuse to appear ungrateful. He's gone through the trouble to rent a studio for me. I won't ruin the moment.

Besides, I want to live in the fantasy.

Before I can reply, my cell goes off in my pocket.

"Sorry," I tell Zander, fishing it out, my fingers fumbling with the tight jeans.

Zander's low, rough chuckle makes my cheeks heat. How does he do this to me? All that warmth leaves me in a sharp wave as I check the screen, my blood running cold.

Seeing the look on my face, Zander asks, "Who is it?" I hear his words, but I don't want to answer. He moves closer to me, invading my space. I feel caught between the two of them. Caught between my past and what could be. It's falling away from me, slipping past my fingertips as the phone rings again in my hand and Zander leans forward.

"Danny," I whisper even though my responding at this point isn't necessary. Zander can see for himself.

"Answer it," Zander says firmly.

"But—" I protest, not wanting this to happen. I don't want to be a part of this anymore.

"Answer it." His words are like stone, hardened by his resolve.

With dread pressing down on my chest, I tap the answer button and put it on speaker.

"Hello?" I ask weakly, although I'm staring at Zander. His eyes aren't on me. His focus is on Danny. I'm lost in the battle between the two of them, back to being nothing but a pawn.

"Where are you?" Danny asks coldly.

I swallow back a nervous lump in my throat. "I'm at home," I answer without thinking, my voice devoid of life.

"Don't lie to me."

I clear my throat and straighten my back. I can't hide from him or my past. "I'm out." He doesn't own me. He's not my Master. *No one is.*

"You're with him," Danny says matter-of-factly. "And you must really think I'm a fucking idiot if you think I think otherwise."

I don't bother arguing.

"I need you to leave him now," Danny tells me firmly in a voice I recognize all too well. One that makes me want to obey. A voice that *made* me obey once upon a time. "Right now. You're no longer his property."

My mouth is dry as I reply, "Danny, I—" Deep down inside of me, I feel the need to tell him no, but as the word climbs up my throat, it's as if I'm being strangled. The word refuses to leave my lips, to be heard by the man who saved me, by the man who beat me. I'm at war with myself and stuck in the middle of a battle between two men.

"I said leave!" Danny screams on the other end of the line, the dark side of him he showed me in the alley coming to the surface. "Or you're as good as fucking dead!"

His jaw clenched tightly, Zander snatches the phone out of my hand, leaving my body trembling on its own.

"Brooks," Zander growls, his voice dropping so low that my skin pricks with more fear than I thought possible at the sound. "If you ever threaten Arianna again, it'll be the last thing you ever do. She's not going anywhere. She's mine. And you're going to pay me the money you owe me. Every. Fucking. Penny. Or you're going to wish I would've killed you back at your office."

Zander hangs up the phone, his eyes blazing with murderous rage. "You'll never speak to him again. He isn't going to touch you."

I don't say a word as a dozen different emotions course

through my body. The threat is very real. My body sways as the shock of what's transpired hits me. *You're as good as fucking dead.* Over and over, his words repeat in my head.

"You're never going back to him," Zander tells me firmly. "Ever."

"What's going to happen?" I ask, my voice barely above a whisper.

"I'm going to make sure he pays," Zander practically growls, tossing the phone onto the end table. It takes a moment for him to look at me, and when he does, his demeanor changes. "You're safe."

He reaches out to me, gripping both of my shoulders and lowering his eyes to mine. "Look at me, sweetheart." I instantly obey him, but I question my instincts. "You're all right, and everything is going to be all right." His words are like a soothing balm, but the wound is too deep.

The only thing I'm truly aware of is that nothing is all right.

CHAPTER 25

ZANDER

There's a gentle breeze outside that blows the light dusting of snow as it falls, twirling before coating the hard ground. It's April and the cold should be moving along, winter done and over, but the chill has lasted longer than it should. I rest my hand against the window. It's cold as ice against my heated body.

He's done.

They're the words I texted Charles. It's long past due for Brooks to be put in his place. Come Monday, there will be nothing left of him.

I turn, looking over my shoulder at Arianna as she wraps her arms around her knees. She's staring into the fire, listening to the crackling as the billows of soft grey smoke spill from between the split logs.

She hasn't been the same. I hate how much control he has over her. How weak he's made her. She keeps saying he saved her, but she has no idea how wrong she is.

"Sweetheart," I call out to her, and she lifts her head from resting on her knees and stares back at me with the desire to be commanded in her eyes. She's lost and scared, just like she was before Brooks got his hands on her. He kept her that way, molded her to believe something else. To believe she was better when he only made her suffer that much more.

I'm going to fix her. It's the only thing I give a damn about anymore.

"I want you to come here," I tell her as I walk to the edge of the rug. She's still on her ass, curled beneath the heat of the fire, but she makes a move to come to me. She nearly crawls. For the split second that she's on all fours, I want her to. The idea of her crawling the few feet and waiting on her knees to please me makes my dick twitch with need. *Soon.* I'm ready to give in, but only once she fully submits. And that starts tonight.

She slowly rises, and I can see in her eyes that she questions if she should have crawled to me. If she wanted to, she should have. It's as simple as that. She'll learn. I'll learn with her. And together, we'll enjoy that depraved darkness we both desire.

"Do you want me?" I ask her. Her eyes spark with fear, the green flecks mixing with a light gold and shining back with panic.

"I . . . yes, I—" she doesn't answer with confidence. Her eyes look down at the plush rug beneath her bare feet.

"You need to know what you want, sweetheart. If you can tell me, I'll give it to you."

"But for how long?" she finally asks the question that's been holding her back. My lips turn up into that smile, the one I love. The one that reflects the happiness she gives me. I brush the stray hairs from her face with the back of my knuckles and lean forward, my hand cupping her chin.

I whisper, my lips nearly touching hers, "However long you'll let me have you."

"I don't want to leave," she tells me with her eyes open, but there's a pain in her voice caused by her confession. Our hot breath mingles as she says, "You make me weak."

The words are like a knife to my heart. If only she knew. I'm the weak one. Only for her.

I press my lips to hers and let my hands roam her body. My fingers trail down to the dip in her waist before I pull back, leaving her to stand on her own, although she almost stumbles.

"Undress for me," I tell her as I grip the ends of my shirt, forcing myself to hold anything other than her. She doesn't hesitate, although her eyes spark with a hint of anger for leaving her in the heat of the moment. The fire crackles and sparks behind her, lighting her with shadows dancing over her slender body as she slowly strips, dropping her clothes to the floor in a puddle at her feet. I do the same, mimicking her movements until we're both naked before each other, bathed in the glow of the fire and nothing else.

"I want you," she whispers, and her simple words

contain so much power. They're so raw and full of a truth that's undeniable.

I step forward, closing the space between us as my toes dig into the plush rug and confess, "I want you, too."

Her lips crash with mine and her fingers spear through my hair as she moans into my mouth. *Yes!* This, this is exactly what I want.

My blunt nails dig into the flesh of her ass as I lift her up, parting her thighs and nestling my dick between her legs as I lower her to the floor beneath us, sinking into the rug in front of the fire.

The soft fur of the rug is nothing like the feel of her skin. So delicate, so easily bruised and broken. But I want her like this. Every part of her moving with me, wanting me just as much as I want her.

I leave open-mouth kisses along her body, over every inch. My hot breath trails along her skin. Her hips buck, and those moans of desperate need fill the air as I toy with her, teasing her just as she's teased me.

"Please." She moans my name. "Zander, please."

She'll never know how much power she gives me when she calls for me like that. When she shows me how much she needs me, how much she craves my touch.

"On all fours." I breathe the command and she's quick to obey, turning over her body, her hair swishing over her shoulder. I let my teeth scrape along her neck before sucking gently at the tender skin in the crook of her neck.

Her plush ass grinds against my cock, begging me to take her and claim her as mine. But this is for her. For her to claim me.

"Take from me, sweetheart." I place my hand on the small of her back as I line my dick up between her hot folds. She's already slick, already wanting me. "Take what you want."

The way she looks at me from over her shoulder teases me to slam into her. To take everything from her and overpower this beautiful creature who's submitted to me.

But there's so much more power in having her take from me.

Her back arches beautifully, her ass rising slightly as she reaches between her legs and grabs a hold of me. A rough groan vibrates up my chest and soothes me as she slowly eases herself backward, her hot cunt taking all of me achingly slowly.

Her hips push back until she's pressed against my groin, her hot cunt filled with my cock. Her forearms brace herself and she leans forward, her head thrashing from side to side as she moves on and off my dick.

My head falls back and my fingers dig into the flesh of her hips. They itch for me to hold her still and fuck her like I want to. But I hold back. Waiting for her.

She rocks herself on and off my dick, her tight cunt sucking me in and making me regret the decision to give her control. My fingers dig deeper, wanting more. Her soft moans turn to ragged breaths as she picks up her pace.

I have to let go of her, warring with the need to take over and pin her down. I fall forward, my hands gripping the rug as her pussy clamps down on my dick. I kiss along her spine, traveling upward and letting her hair tickle my nose as she cums violently, urging me to spill myself deep inside her as her body trembles with the shock of her orgasm.

A cold sweat breaks out over my body, and I finally feel like I can breathe. Her body sags on the floor, limp and sated, but I'm not done with her.

"Good girl," I tell her before nipping her earlobe and propping her back up and onto all fours. She turns to look at me over her shoulder, her breathing frantic.

My hands are gentle as I trail them down her back, catching my breath and positioning my knees so I can take her hard and fast. I only give her a moment, only waiting to see her lower her front to the floor to steady herself and then look back at me with her mouth parted.

I slam into her, buried to the hilt without any mercy as she screams out. I piston my hips, taking her over and over with a relentless pace.

I'm already close to cumming. The sight of her taking pleasure from me was enough to be my undoing. Her fingers dig into the carpet and her pussy spasms on my cock. "Zander!" she screams out my name as I pound into her over and over. My toes curl and the very bottom of my spine tingles as I thrust my hips once, twice, and one last time before cumming deep inside her.

My body falls forward as she shakes beneath me, the

waves of her own release racing through her. My hand grips hers as my body covers hers and I kiss her shoulder tenderly.

"Never question whether I want you," I tell her softly. "Never question whether you're mine."

She breathes out heavily, strands of hair falling in her face. Her gorgeous eyes stare back at me and she answers, "Yes, Zander," as I kiss her shoulder one last time.

CHAPTER 26

ARIANNA

The crackle of spent logs and the scent of wood smoke fill the room as Zander slips on his dark blazer over his white dress shirt and adjusts his cufflinks in one smooth flourish. I bite my lower lip as I watch him check out his freshly shaven appearance in the bedroom mirror. He has to know that he looks good. This is just habit.

After adjusting his black tie, he turns around, his piercing blue eyes focusing on me.

My skin pricks as the intensity of his stare summons a dull ache between my thighs, a reminder of the passionate night before.

"You'll be fine while I'm gone?" Zander asks me, giving me his boyish grin that makes my heart skip a beat.

I grip the grey silk bathrobe in my hands, pulling it tighter around my chest. "I think so," I say. I pause, not knowing if I should pry, but hesitantly ask, "Where are you going?"

Zander's grin quietly fades. "I have some business to take care of."

I want to ask him what kind, but I stop myself. There's a reason he keeps his secrets, and maybe he doesn't trust me with them yet. But he can't keep them from me forever.

He can too, says an annoying voice at the back of my head. *This is all pretend.*

Fuck you, I want to tell the voice. I don't need any negativity shitting on my rainbow right now. I just want to be happy for once.

I shove down my anxiety and ask, "Do you know when you'll be back?"

Zander raises his right hand to glance down at his platinum Rolex. "I think around six. I'll bring back dinner."

Damn, that's a long time. What the hell will I do until then?

I try to keep my disappointment from showing, but I barely manage. "Okay."

Zander crosses the space between us, hooking his hand beneath my chin and tilting my head back to force me to look into his eyes. "Don't be sad, sweetheart," he says softly. "I have something for you to do while I'm gone."

"What?" I ask, my mind racing with what it could be.

His boyish grin grows wider. "I bought an easel and painting supplies for you so you could work here when you're not in the studio. I set it all up in the piano room."

A feeling of warmth goes through my chest, and I stand on my tiptoes to give him a kiss on the lips. "Thank you," I breathe with gratitude when I pull away. My cheeks hurt from the wide smile on my face, but I don't even try to hide it.

Zander winks at me. "I thought you might like it." He gives me several more kisses that leave me wanting more before pulling away. There's a look of regret on his face as he gazes at me, as if he wishes he could stay. "Don't go anywhere while I'm gone, and do not answer your phone if you don't know who it is. I don't want you in contact with *him*."

I nod my head slowly, my anxiety slightly rising at his serious tone. "I won't." I promise. It's not like Danny's threat feels real, it doesn't. But I feel safer here with Zander. I don't want to see Danny at all. Just the thought makes a chill run through my body. I don't want to talk to him. I don't want anything to do with him, and I trust Zander when he says he's taking care of it.

Zander gives me one more quick kiss on the lips. "Later then, sweetheart."

He walks over to the door, but before he can leave, I call out, "Wait."

Zander turns, arching an eyebrow in question.

"What am I supposed to paint while you're gone?"

His brow furrows in thought for a moment and then he gives me that boyish grin. "I don't know. Surprise me."

With a wink, he's gone, leaving me alone in the room. I listen to the sound of his footsteps receding down the hallway until they fade into the distance. After a minute, I hear the roar of the engine of one of his cars start up outside as he drives away.

I chew on my lip, wondering what I could paint for Zander. Looking around the room, I feel like he has expensive taste. Hmm . . . an item of wealth, maybe? Power? I shake my head. No, I don't think he'd like that.

I got it! Remembering his reaction to my painting of the woman, I suddenly have an idea and my face breaks out into an excited grin. My fingers itching with excitement, I rush out into the hall toward the piano room. I stop just outside, grabbing the picture frame off the stand just outside the door.

When I walk into the room, the breath catches in my throat.

"Oh," I say softly, butterflies in my stomach.

Zander's set up a chair and easel on the dais with the piano, pointing it toward the floor-to-ceiling windows so I could paint with the breathtaking backdrop in front of me. He even went to the trouble to have the painting supplies set out and ready. All I have to do is sit down and start painting.

This is so sweet of him. So unexpected.

Tears pricking my eyes, I walk up the dais and set the frame upright on the piano. I take a seat at the easel and look at the brushes. When I choose the right one, I dip it into a deep earth tone shade of brown and begin painting.

Over the next several hours, I lose all sense of time as I work on the painting, frequently casting glances at the picture frame, trying to get every detail and nuance right. I don't take any breaks, and I get so lost in my art, not even getting up to go to the bathroom. And by the time I'm close to done, my back is aching and my right hand feels nearly numb.

"Almost there," I whisper, setting a brush down into a small cup of water on the stand next to me. There's a bit of paint on Zander's shirt I'm wearing, but I'm sure he won't mind. I fucking hope not. "It's missing something," I murmur, staring hard at the painting, a replica of Zander's mother, Marie.

I stare at it long and hard, trying to figure out what it is. Finally, I snap my fingers.

Her smile. A feeling of joy sweeps through me, a rush of euphoria I always get when I'm close to finishing a work of art. It's not quite right. There's life to the smile I see in the photo. A tenderness that shows her love for Zander. And it's missing from this canvas.

"Once I get that done," I say happily, loving how it all looks, "it'll be perfect."

And I hope Zander will love it.

I'm about to pick up a paintbrush and apply the finishing touches when I hear a faint ringing sound. I pause, frowning, straining my ears. I can't tell exactly where the sound is coming from, but it sounds like it's in the other room.

I pick the paintbrush back up, but now that I've heard the sound, I can't unhear it. I've got to know what it is. Sighing, I place the paintbrush down and walk into the adjoining room, one of Zander's studies.

Ding. Ding. Ding.

It's my cell, lying on his desk.

When I see the messages on the screen, my heart leaps up my throat.

It's Natalie. Fuck!

I've been so worried about Danny that I forgot to call her.

That's not true, says the annoying voice at the back of my head. *You were too wrapped up with your lover, Zander, to care.*

I'm really starting to hate that fucking voice right now, especially because it reminds me how much of a shitty friend I've been.

Sucking in a deep breath, I pick up the phone, reading through some of the messages.

Nattybatty95: Hey Ari! I got some crazy shit to tell you! I can't wait to get home to talk to you about it :P

Nattybatty95: Where you at, chica?

Nattybatty95: Is something wrong? :(

Nattybatty95: Why aren't you home yet?

Nattybatty95: WTF

Nattybatty95: I'm filing a missing persons report if I don't hear from you within the next day

The last message sends me into a panic and my fingers are flying across the keys before I even have time to process.

Artistchick96: Hey Nat! Don't go filing a police report!!! I'm totally fine! Don't worry. I just took a mini-vacation, that's all

My cell chimes with an immediate *ding*.

Nattybatty95: Ari! Thank God you're all right! I was just about to file that report on you

Thank fuck she didn't. Jesus.

Artistchick96: No need! I'm okay.

Nattybatty95: Holy shit, you scared me to death! I thought you'd been kidnapped or something

My fingers fly across the touch screen.

Artistchick96: Nope. You're still stuck with me.

Nattybatty95: Wait, where are you? And where the hell have you been!?

I pause before responding, biting my lower lip while I think. I feel awful about the worry and panic I've caused Natalie. And I can't believe I haven't thought to send her a message while I've been staying over here with Zander. But deep down, I know a part of me didn't want to contact Natalie because . . . I knew she'd be trouble.

If I told her I was staying somewhere, she would've pestered me with endless questions.

God, I feel awful.

Sucking in a deep breath, I type out a quick message, ignoring her last message.

Artistchick96: hey . . . are you home?

Nattybatty95: No, but I will be in about a half hour.

Nattybatty95: Why what's up?

I hesitate, my heart pounding in my chest. As bad as I feel about keeping Nat in the dark, I'm not sure if I want to do this. *But if I don't give her at least something, she might grow suspicious.*

Artistchick96: I want to meet up. To talk about something.

I'm barely done pressing send when the screen lights up with another *ding*.

Nattybatty95: I'd definitely be down for that. Burning rubber to get home.

Artistchick96: See u there

Another *ding*.

Nattybatty95: What's this all about? Is it Danny?

I turn off the phone instead of answering. It'll take too much to type to tell my story, and I'd rather think about what I'm going to tell her on the way over. I still haven't decided if I'm going to tell her the truth yet or make up some story.

But whatever I'm gonna do, I need to go there quickly so I can get back before Zander's home. Glancing at the clock on the wall, it's almost one, so I don't have too long, but it's still plenty of time.

Don't leave here without telling me. His words echo in my mind before I can take a single step.

For a moment, I'm frozen with indecision, not sure what to do. Zander was explicit about not going anywhere without asking for his permission.

But Natalie's my friend. And she needs to see me to feel secure. I can't leave her worrying about me like that.

Deciding that Zander will have to get over it if he finds out, I quickly get dressed and take off without looking back. He'll get over it. I glance at my purse a few times, wondering if I should text him. But I don't. Instead, I turn up the radio and try to relax, but it's impossible.

A heavy weight settles on my chest just thinking about opening up to Natalie. I don't know what I should do. Tell the truth? Or lie.

There are no pros to either one. I tell the truth and Natalie goes nuts, wanting to call the police. I tell a lie, and I feel like a shit-face asshole.

I lose either way.

Whatever I do, I'm still going to apologize for being an absentee friend these past few months. It's really not fair how I've treated her after all she's done for me.

When I pull into my usual parking space at the apartments, I don't see Natalie's car anywhere, but I figure she'll show up any minute as I step out of the car and head up inside. The familiar scent of Natalie's perfume hits me as I step through the doorway and I feel a sense of nostalgia.

I've been so wrapped up with Zander, I forgot how much I've missed my friends these past few days.

I walk down the hallway and go into my room. I toss the keys on my dresser and head over to the closet to grab some more canvas, but before I can open the doors, my eyes are drawn to a note on my bed.

My stomach drops in my chest when I pick it up and read it.

> *Ari,*
>
> *I know I haven't been the best friend to you lately, always bugging you about the problems you're having with Danny, but I'd just like to tell you I'm concerned about your well-being. I don't mean to be intrusive when I'm trying to figure out what's going on. I just care about you and want what's best for you. I really do hope that you'll tell me about your problems one day.*
>
> *Until then,*
>
> *Love always,*
>
> *Crazy Nat*

Tears sting the back of my eyes as I read the message.

"Oh, Nat," I say softly, swallowing back a large lump in my throat, "Why do you have to make this *so* damn hard?" Now I'm *really* dreading our conversation. A part of me wants to leave now before she comes back so I don't have to deal with the situation. But I'm not going to take the easy way out. I'm going to wait until she's here to decide which action I take.

I reread the message several more times before placing it on my nightstand and walking back into the living room to wait for Nat.

I flip through channels on the TV, thinking Nat is going to walk through the door any minute. But almost thirty minutes later, she's still not here. I glance at the time, my anxiety growing. Zander said he'd be back at six, and it's almost two.

I turn back on my phone to text Nat to see what's going on. Before I can type a letter, the last message she sent before I turned my cell off pops up.

Nattybatty95: Hey I'm going to stop by A.C. Moore to get some supplies so we can chat while we paint. I have a feeling this is gonna be a juicy talk. ;)

Artistchick96: Okay. I'm here at the apt already . . . but can you hurry? I need to leave here by 5:30.

No sooner than I'm done texting, there's a knock at the door.

My heart jumps in my chest, my hand gripping at my shirt. *It's Natalie.* It has to be. She's probably back with her hands full of painting supplies. I let out a breath and try to shake off the dread.

Knock. Knock. Knock.

"Coming," I call, slowly getting up and moving as fast as I can.

I take a deep breath when I place my hand on the door

handle. Muttering a quick prayer, I swing the door open and put on a cheery smile, "Hey, Nat—"

My heart freezes as I see Danny standing only a foot away with a demented grin on his face. He's dressed in his usual dress pants and dress shirt, except his eyes are bloodshot, his hair isn't finely coiffed as usual, and his clothes look rumpled.

"Expecting someone else?" he sneers. A whiff of alcohol hits me, and I immediately know he's been drinking.

"Danny?" I gasp. "What are you doing here?" It's hard not to tremble and keep my voice even. I wasn't expecting this at all. Zander's words come to me unbidden.

Don't leave the house without telling me.

"I've come to collect my debt," he growls, his eyes boring into me with a hatred that causes my skin to prick.

"What? What are you talking about?" I try to move, to slam the door in his face, but my body feels frozen, paralyzed with fear. He takes enough of a step in that I can't slam the door. *I can run though.*

"I followed you here," he says, his voice low and dangerous.

"You know what?" I ask after swallowing the lump growing in my throat and being as firm as I can manage, "You're making me feel uncomfortable. I think you should leave." It's hard, standing up for myself. But I don't have to take this kind of abuse from Danny. Not anymore. My hand feels hot as I push slightly on the door.

"You're really asking me to leave?" Danny demands in disbelief, his nostrils flaring as he splays his hand on the door, keeping it from shutting.

"You've been drinking," I say, "and you don't look well. It's for the best." My heart beats chaotically. If I just act like everything's fine, it'll be okay. I'm in control. "Please leave." I hold his gaze, straightening my back and willing him to go and leave me alone.

For a moment, I think Danny is going to comply with my wishes, his head bowing. But when he looks back up at me, my blood runs cold.

"I don't think so," he says, his voice dark and deadly. Without warning, he rushes forward.

Crying out in alarm, I try to slam the door, but it smacks against his foot and he forces it open with a feral grunt. The door hits me straight on and I stumble, falling onto the floor. Heart pounding like a hammer, I scramble forward on my hands and knees while simultaneously reaching for my cell in my pocket.

I open my mouth, preparing to scream as loud as I can. But cold, powerful hands clamp down on my mouth from behind, muffling my cries. His hard body falls on top of me, knocking the phone out of my hand, but I grab it, forcing it into my blouse to hold onto it.

Kicking and bucking, I struggle violently, but I'm no match for Danny's strength. He presses down hard on my neck, cutting off my air supply. I strain against his grasp, my heart pounding so hard I think it will burst. Danny increases the pressure, growling in my ear like the monster he is.

I grow weak, my vision dimming black around the edges.

It only takes about five seconds for me to go limp.

"I gave you to him," I hear Danny's voice growl from somewhere far away as I fade off into darkness. "But now I'm taking you back."

CHAPTER 27

ZANDER

"You look like shit."

I look up at Charles and see him smile. Grunting a humorless laugh, I lean forward and toss the papers back to him.

"I guess that's what happens when you get your hands dirty," he says with a glint in his eyes.

"You couldn't be happier, could you?" I ask him.

"Just surprised you risked your pretty boy face," he says with a smirk.

"You're not the only one," I mutter beneath my breath. My father hasn't let it go. *Everyone knows*. I'm a disgrace. Or so my father tells me. I haven't responded to him, and I won't. He'll never understand. She's worth more than anything. She's worth far more than my reputation. If my father could understand that, my mother may still be breathing.

"What's going on with her?" Charles asks me, catching my attention with his tone.

"What do you mean?" My heart races a little faster with him questioning me about her. I don't want anyone to question it.

"The money—" he starts to ask, and I cut him off. I'm so fucking sick of talking about money. So much fucking money runs through my hands. I don't need it. I'm tired of chasing it. I just want to live a full life. One with her.

"I'll give her the money, but it's not going to him. It's just for her." My voice is flat but firm.

"So, it's just the month?" Charles asks.

My stomach drops at his question. She said she doesn't want to leave me and I believe her, but only time will tell if she's actually happy. If I can give her enough. "I'd rather it not be."

His brow raises as he leans back in his seat, the leather groaning. "It seems . . . expensive."

I shrug, not knowing what to say.

"How do the contracts work?" Charles asks.

"It's just a month," I explain, and my voice is flat. "After that, I'm keeping her."

"Paying?" he asks, resting his ankle on his knee and tapping his foot.

"No." I'm harsh with my answer, narrowing my eyes. He raises his hands defensively. "She's not a whore," I say, and I practically spit the words. Is it too much to think she'd want me without my money? I don't entertain the thought. I refuse to think she'd leave me. She's not in it for the money. She'll stay when the contract is over. I'll make sure of it. Whatever she desires, I'll give it to her. I'll spend every cent of my wealth on her to keep her happy.

"I'm just asking out of curiosity."

I'm about to tell him to mind his own business when he adds, "They're an interesting thing, the auctions."

I glance at the screen on the computer as he talks. The living room is empty, the house quiet and cold without her in it.

"I imagine a woman would put herself up for auction . . . if she knew about it."

I check the cameras to the house again, but Arianna's not home yet. She knows to be home when I get back. My only request is that she greet me when I get home. If I had it my way, she'd never leave, but I'm not so selfish to think that's possible.

"Your sweetheart isn't home yet?" Charles asks me, and there's a slight mocking tone in his voice. I just give him a sharp look and don't say anything.

"It's different, seeing you like this," he says.

"Like what?" Weak. I've never felt as though Charles was an enemy, but his tone makes me question.

His answer surprises me. "Like you give a fuck."

I stare at him, searching his face for his intentions, but I don't have to guess.

"I'm jealous," Charles admits and then looks away, staring past me and out to the window behind me. The dark night of the city sky plays shadows across his face.

"Jealous?" I ask him, a smile creeping onto my lips.

"Not jealous of your face," Charles answers with a smirk. I huff a laugh and lean back in my seat.

"It's good to see you happy," Charles says with a lowered voice. I meet his eyes, and I know with everything in me that he's being genuine.

I prefer not to let the emotions dictate my response. I shake them off, leaning back in my seat and resting my chin in my hand. "I'll be happy when Brooks is out of the picture."

"Changing the subject," Charles says, the grin fading from his lips. It's quiet a moment until he answers, "Soon."

"When is it happening?" I ask him as I pick up the slate block, and the edges seem sharper to me than they ever have before.

Charles shrugs. "It all depends on what you'd like." He takes out his phone, tapping the screen and bringing up Brooks's information. "He's predictable. If you'd like it to look natural, that can be arranged. I suppose it just depends on when and where."

I nod my head once, debating on what to respond, but Charles interrupts me. "We have a problem."

There's an urgency in his voice that makes me sit up

straighter. I wait for him to continue as he watches the phone, his body stiff.

"Where's Arianna?" he asks me.

"She should be at my place s—"

"He was at her place. He changed his routine. He went to her house."

My hands grip the edge of the desk. "He's on Fourth Street?" There's only one reason that Brooks would go there. I take out my own phone and message Arianna to text me back and stare at the screen, willing her to text me, but nothing comes.

I can't wait. "When was he there?" I ask Charles, my voice fighting to hold back the panic I feel. She's been gone for hours. My thumb taps across my phone and I call her. The phone rings and rings, but there's no answer. Everything in me stills. He's gotten to her.

Charles nods his head as he taps on the screen of his phone. "Three hours ago." I hang up the phone and realize that's right when she left. *He was watching her.* I call her again. Ring. Ring. Ring.

"Where is he now?" I ask him as my ice-cold blood slowly pumps through my veins.

"His place."

"On Andrews?" I confirm, already grabbing my keys off the desk and leaving for the door.

"Yeah," Charles says as he grabs his coat and comes up behind me.

"He has her. I know it."

Charles nods his head, throwing on his coat as I open the door.

"You're coming?" I ask him.

He nods his head once, the mask of indifference on his face morphing as he smiles at me. "I can't let you have all the fun." His humor does nothing to ease me. Right now, nothing will make me feel as though I haven't already lost her.

"We'll get her back, Zander," he tells me as he places a hand on my shoulder.

I don't answer him. The door closes behind us as I stalk to the elevator with purposeful strides. I'm not letting him take her. I'll kill him first.

CHAPTER 28

ARIANNA

Whoosh!

The sound of the whip sings through the air before lashing against my bare back. *Crack!*

A strangled scream rips from my throat, echoing in the hollow basement as blazing pain shoots up and down my flesh. I weakly struggle against my bonds, sweat beading my brow. I'm suspended, naked, held up by chains hanging from the ceiling.

It's useless to fight. My head lolls to the side as my aching body screams at me to do something, yet I'm too weak. I never had a chance. I woke up in this position, and every ounce of my body is sore from fighting.

Despair consumes me.

The only thing I feel is pain.

I scream and scream again until my voice is raw and cracking, shaking against my bonds, my back on fire.

After several agonizing moments, my head drops forward and I hang limply, my limbs trembling as my body breaks out in a cold sweat. I don't know if he's going to hit me again, but I don't even know if I'll feel it, my vision blackening around the edges.

"I gave you everything," Danny says behind me, his boots thudding against the cement floor as he paces behind me, his voice filled with utter contempt.

My eyelids open at the sound of his voice. He hasn't spoken since I woke up. My voice is sore from screaming, from begging and pleading. I can feel the cool air blowing over the open lashes, and it stings with a pain that's indescribable, but even that isn't enough to scream over. The only movements, the only sounds I have the energy for are those that are instinctual. And even then, they're dulled by exhaustion.

I lick my dry, cracked lips. "Danny . . . please," my voice croaks as I cry weakly, tears streaming down my hot face. "You don't have to do this." I think I say the words, but my eyes are so heavy, my body so weak and the pain so unbearable, I'm not certain of anything.

"He wants to keep you?" Danny asks angrily.

I swallow back the lump of fear in my throat as I try to think of a response. I clench my sweaty hands, my fingers brushing against the rough metal, and the raw cuts at the sharp cuffs shoot a pain down my arms that makes me wince.

"And you want him to, don't you?" Danny's words are just a whisper. His voice is eerily calm. I try to pick my head up, my throat too dry to answer.

I hear him drop the whip. My heart slams in my chest and my body stiffens. I think that's what I heard. Please, God, please. I can't take any more.

"Well, he can have you back," Danny whispers next to my ear. His breath feels so cold. Everything feels so cold. "As soon as I'm done with you," Danny says as he wraps my hair around his wrist and pulls my head back too sharply, a scream tearing through me as my neck is ripped to the side.

The moment he lets go, I hear him pick the whip back up, and somehow, I'm able to cry again. Not that it will do me any good. I can't save myself. I'm powerless and pathetic.

Dread presses down on my chest as his whip sings through the air and I cringe. *Whoosh! Crack!*

Whoosh!

Crack!

Whoosh!

Crack!

My mouth opens wide in agony, saliva dripping from my lips, but I have no voice left to scream with. I buck, shudder, and strain against my bindings, my back feeling like it's being flayed to the bone.

With each painful lash, the room spins around me, my breathing becoming shallow, ragged.

My heart is becoming sluggishly slow.

When the darkness finally claims me, I'm incredibly grateful. I only pray it will swallow me whole.

CHAPTER 29

ZANDER

"If the cops had seen—" He won't fucking let it go. I sped the whole way here. He's had her for nearly four hours. Four fucking hours.

"Enough," I snap at Charles. He won't shut the fuck up. I get out of my car which I've parked a block down from Brooks's house and slam the door.

"You need to be quiet," Charles says and grabs me, gripping my shoulder and slamming me against the car.

All I can see is red.

I push against him, but he pushes me back.

"He has her!" I scream at him, but he doesn't relent, slamming my head into the car and pushing his face against mine.

"Calm the fuck down," he says through clenched teeth. I wish he hadn't come with me.

I use all of my weight and push him off me. He stumbles backward and nearly falls on his ass.

"He's going to see you coming."

"Let him!" I scream, my voice hoarse and my skin so fucking hot I can barely stand it. I just need her back. I turn from him and take quick strides, my eyes focused on the house at the end of the barren street.

"He could kill her," Charles calls out to me, and it's only then that I pause. My heart freezes in my chest. No. I clench my teeth and move my hand to the gun at my waistband. I hear Charles's footsteps walk up behind me slowly, with determined steps. "If you barge in, he could kill her."

I'm silent as I stand there, feeling a wave of nausea threatening to come up.

"We both know he didn't take her for a chat."

"Stop it," I tell him with my eyes closed. All I can see is her face, her smile. I can practically hear her laugh.

"You need to listen to me. You need to restrain yourself."

My hands ball into fists and my blunt nails dig into the fleshy part of my palm. "Just go then. Lead the way, but no more waiting. I need her."

Charles slaps a hand on my back, and it's hard and firm. He moves ahead of me, and I lift my eyes to watch his back as he moves off the sidewalk and hides in the shadows of the trees along the large estates.

He looks over his shoulder, and I'm quick to move, my heart pounding so hard it's the only thing I can hear.

Thud. Thud. Thud. Each beat is another second she's in there with him.

I can't hear a damn thing. A loud ringing in my ears is the only thing I can focus on as Charles leads me through the scattered trees to the side of Brooks's house.

I don't even realize he's picking the lock until I try to shove him away. I just need to get to her.

I can feel it in the pit of my stomach. He's hurting her. He has for years, but now it's personal. I stand there watching Charles shoving the pick into the lock and twist it slightly before I hear a muffled scream.

The blood drains from my face, and ice replaces my blood as Charles's eyes meet mine.

"Open it," I mouth the words to him. My hand slowly travels to the cold steel of my gun. My reddened vision becomes focused. Adrenaline is bringing life to the hatred burning inside me.

The door clicks and slowly opens, and I move in front of Charles. He doesn't stop me as I move through the house. The floorboards are creaking loudly under my weight. I don't stop. All I can hear is that scream, her pain. It compels me to go to her, a pull so strong, so violent that nothing can stop me. Nothing will keep me from her or save him from death.

She screams again as I come to a stop in the narrow hallway to a heavy door with an old steel knob. I test it and the knob turns easily, her scream louder as I creak it open.

My heart pounds in my chest as I hear the swish of a whip and the crack of it against her skin. The lights are dim as I move down the stairs, my gun held out in front of me.

Time slows as I see her, hanging there from the chains with him behind her. Pure hatred shines in his eyes as he pulls the heavy whip back over his shoulder, ready to strike her again.

It only takes two shots. *Bang! Bang!*

He wavers on his feet, staring down at his chest where the small holes in his chest seem to vanish, but blood quickly seeps through the fabric and spreads along the woven threads.

I keep my arm up, the kick of the gun still traveling up my arm as he falls to his knees first, his head tilting back up to me, his forehead pinching and his hands moving to his chest. It's not long before he falls forward, his face slamming against the ground, his body lifeless.

My feet move down the steps, going closer to him. I don't take my eyes off him as I empty the gun into his skull. *Bang! Bang! Bang!*

I keep pulling the trigger even after it's empty. His dead eyes are open and staring back at me as blood pools around his disfigured face.

It's only the sound of her whimper that tears me away from him.

"Don't touch her!" I scream at Charles, making him flinch as he puts both his hands up.

There's so much blood. Lashes mar her back, her shoulders, her thighs. Everywhere. He tore her flesh open. I don't hesitate to pick her small body up, relieving the weight that's pulling her wrists against the metal cuffs.

"Zander," she says, and her voice is so weak as her head droops to the side.

"It's all right," I tell her quickly as Charles works on the locks at her wrist. He must've found the key somewhere, because they're off in an instant. Her arms are falling like dead weight and making her face twist in pain.

She cries out as I turn her body, cradling it and feeling the warmth of her blood soaking into my shirt and against my arms.

"Here," Charles says and passes me a white sheet. I question using it for only a moment before wrapping it around her body, not tightly. Every small movement makes her wince with pain.

"Talk to me, Arianna," I tell her. Her eyes look as if she's staring far off into the distance. "Arianna," my voice cracks as I say her name.

I'm too late.

"We need to get out of here," Charles says as he looks around the cellar. My shoes have traveled through the blood, tracking footprints wherever I've been. "I need to call for a clean up."

My heart races as I realize what's happened. What I've done.

"Hopefully, there's time," Charles says so softly I'm not sure I was meant to hear him.

My body shakes as I hold her closer to me, carrying her weak body up the steps and letting Charles lead the way. "I've got you," I whisper, kissing her hair. "It's all right," I tell her even though I'm not sure it is. My body is so cold, so numb.

Sirens scream in the background as we walk away from the house.

"We should have gotten the silencer," Charles mutters beneath his breath, opening the car door for me.

We would have had time to clean up. Time to hide the evidence if we had stopped to get his equipment like he'd told me to.

Arianna groans with pain in my arms, the blood seeping through the thin white sheet.

But then my sweetheart might not have survived.

CHAPTER 30

ARIANNA

I groan softly with the twinge of pain as the doctor works on mending my back. My hands fist the comforter and my head thrashes from side to side. I'm on pain meds, but the prodding and stitches bring sharp pains that won't go away. I'm alive though. "Zander," I croak, barely able to force the words from my lips. I try to be still, feeling the cool air sting my open wounds, but it's hard. It just *hurts*. I've never felt so much pain in my life.

In the background, I hear heavy footsteps softened by plush carpet coming toward the bed. As the footsteps get closer, I lift my head to see Zander, his face a tortured mask. But my movement proves to be a mistake as horrible pain runs up and down my back. I suck in a sharp breath through clenched teeth, trying my best not to cry out. I don't want him to see me like this, but I need him here. I just want him to hold me.

A large but gentle hand touches my shoulder where there aren't any wounds.

"Don't move," Zander says, his voice low and sounding like a soft rebuke.

It hurts me to hear that tone in his voice. "I'm sorry," I tell Zander quietly, my face pressed against the mattress, my lips mashed together. I'm sorry I ever left. I'm sorry I couldn't fight harder. I'm ashamed. I brought all of this on Zander. And now Danny's blood is on Zander's hands. Guilt mixes with anxiety in my stomach, making me feel sick.

"It's all right," I hear Zander reply, his voice softer now. Even through my pain, a warmth flows through my chest.

"I should've listened to you," I say remorsefully. *And none of this would've happened.*

"It's going to be all right," Zander repeats. He crouches down so his eyes are level with mine.

My heart skips a beat at his handsome face so close to mine, his masculine scent calming me. His gaze pierces through me, his heavenly blue eyes clouded with emotion.

I attempt a smile as Zander leans in, pressing his lips against mine, his hand cupping my jaw while his thumb rubs soothing circles on my cheek, causing my skin to warm from just his touch alone. But he murdered someone. I heard what Charles said. There wasn't time to hide anything. They're going to know. They're going to come for him. I'll tell them everything. They can't blame Zander. They can't . . . I can hardly breathe, and the reality makes me dizzy with agony. "Is it going to be okay?" I whisper against Zander's lips, my heart in my throat, my eyes shut from the pain. *Please tell me that it is. Please tell me that everything is going to be okay.*

"Everything's going to be fine," he says softly.

My eyes flutter open and I see his piercing blue eyes gazing at me. His jaw is clenched, his expression conflicted.

I look back at him, my heart still in my throat. I have the sudden urge to tell him that I love him. That I want to be with him forever. He really saved me. I truly owe him my life.

But I can't find the strength to speak the words as I watch the look in his eyes change.

Deep down, I know that he's lying to me.

Everything isn't going to be okay. And it's all because of me.

CHAPTER 31

ZANDER

I wish I could just pause time. If only it were possible. The soft sounds of Arianna sleeping peacefully are the only sounds I concentrate on. If I don't, all I can hear is the bang of my gun. The thud of his body hitting the floor. The sound of her screams.

I close my eyes, wishing the image would go away. It's not the blood from the bullet holes spilling onto the floor that makes my stomach turn with sickness, it's Ariana's blood stained on the cement under her and caked on her back.

I grit my teeth, my hands fisting the sheets as I try to contain the anger.

A soft moan makes me open my eyes as Arianna twists on the bed, nestling closer to me and giving me a warmth I'm in desperate need of.

Her small hand meets my chest, and instantly, her body relaxes and she moves closer in her sleep as I put my arms over her waist.

Her simple touch calms the anger inside me. I feel raw and powerless with her next to me. I'd do anything for her. She turns me away from everything I've ever known. It means nothing compared to her touch.

I've sacrificed it all. I already know I'm going down for this. Charles messaged me this morning that there's too much evidence. Video surveillance from the gala, her blood, his blood.

We both knew it as I stood over Brooks's dead body. There was no going back. No hiding it. I'm only biding my time until they come for me.

If only I could pause this moment and stay with her forever.

"Mmm," Arianna's soft voice brings my eyes to hers. They flutter open and she yawns, covering her mouth with her hand. As she moves her arm, she winces, a reminder of the pain from the wounds on her back.

I wish I could do more for her. I feel like I failed her. *In so many ways, I have.*

"How do you feel?" I ask, but my voice croaks and I have to clear my throat. I haven't slept, and that's evident in my voice. My eyes feel heavy and my body is begging for me to let go, but I can't. I know I only have a few moments left with her. I won't waste them sleeping.

"Okay," Arianna answers me, her hand moving to the stubble on my jaw. I take her hand in mine and kiss her palm, making that sweet smile form on her face. I love that smile. It should always be there. She deserves that happiness.

"Do you need any more meds?" I ask her, my eyes automatically flashing to the clock. It's nearly eight. She can't have another dose for two more hours.

"I'm fine," she says with the soft smile still there. "Really." She leans forward and hides the pain that's clearly there to kiss me on the lips.

I don't waste the moment. I pull her closer to me, holding onto her small body carefully and gently and deepening the kiss. I part her lips with my tongue, slipping it along the seam and then stroking her tongue with mine. Our tongues mingle in a dark dance of desperate need. Her moans fill my hot mouth as she pushes herself against me. Her breasts press against my chest, and her leg brushes over my knee.

I nip her bottom lip and look down at her. Her dark eyes look up through her thick lashes and her lips part. Our hot breath fills the air between us.

A moment passes with a spark igniting between us. Not lust, something stronger. *So much stronger.* Her lips part, and she almost has a chance to say the words, but I don't let her. I push my lips against hers, muffling anything she could say and putting every ounce of passion and need into my touch.

I can't bear to say it, knowing how this ends, but I hope she can feel it. That's all I need. As long as she can feel it, it'll stay with her forever.

As I break the kiss, I hear the banging on the front door. My heart freezes, but it's not from knowing that I'm done. That I'll be in jail soon and on the stand for murder. It's not the threat of life behind bars or the death penalty that makes my heart stop. It's the look in Arianna's eyes and the way her nails dig into my arm as I pull away from her.

"No," Arianna whispers, her head shaking as I move off the bed, ignoring her attempt to keep me with her in the safety and warmth of the comforter.

"I have to," I tell her with my back to her. I'm not going to run. I know that's not an option. I take in a breath as the bed groans and Arianna grabs her sweater off the floor, throwing it on and ignoring the pain she must be feeling and running through the hall to catch up to me. Her bare feet pad on the floor as a voice says through the door, "Zander Payne, open up! We have a warrant!"

"Go back to bed, Arianna," I command her, but she doesn't listen.

I clench my teeth as the banging of a fist on the other side of the door echoes in the foyer.

"Zander." Arianna pulls on my arm, begging me to look at her. She swallows thickly, looking at the door as the banging continues.

"Sweetheart," I tell her with the semblance of a smile on my face. "It's okay," I lie to her. It hurts to do it. "Just go back to bed," I say, and my voice cracks. I brush the hair away from her face and cup her chin.

Bang! The knock at the door sounds so much louder.

"Coming!" I call out, and at my voice, Arianna hunches forward, tears falling down her cheeks.

I lean down and kiss her lips, tasting the salt before

resting the tip of my nose against hers. "You'll be all right," I tell her in a soft voice. It's meant to comfort her, but it only forces a sob from her throat.

She cries quietly behind me in the middle of the foyer as I unlock the door and open it, stepping aside. Each beat of my heart seems slower.

Four cops stand at my doorstep, the first pushing the door open wider as he steps through.

"Zander Payne?" the man asks. He has dark skin and dark eyes to match. Tall and broad shouldered, his voice doesn't match the intimidation of his presence. The man is deadly, that much is obvious, but his voice is calm and level. Professional even. "I'm Officer Richter, and this is Officer Lawson."

I nod my head, meeting his eyes and waiting for the arrest.

The man behind him, Officer Lawson, comes in with cuffs already out. "Turn around, sir. We have a warrant for your arrest." The second officer speaks this time, a much shorter man with tanned skin but lacking the same forceful presence as the first man. His voice still echoes authority though. And I listen, turning around and putting my hands behind my back.

I don't ask what I'm being arrested for. Maybe I should. I should have prepared this better. But the truth is, she was never a part of my plans. None of this was supposed to happen.

"Zander," Ariana's voice is full of pain as the metal brushes against my skin. It's cold, and the clinking of the cuffs is loud as the metal closes around my wrists. A strong hand rests on my shoulders as I'm pushed against the wall. My cheek is flat against the drywall as the man pats me down.

"You have the right to remain silent. If you do say anything, it can be used against you in a court of law. You have the right to have a lawyer present during any—"

"I did it!" Arianna calls out. I can't see her with my face still pressed against the wall. My eyes pop open, and my heart races as her words hit me. I try pushing back against the man holding me, but his hold is unforgiving.

"I killed Daniel Brooks. I did it!" Ariana shrieks and runs forward, toward the cops. I can hear the commotion behind me. I push against the man holding me, and this time I'm forceful. "I shot him. I can tell you everything. Please don't take him."

"Keep quiet!" I yell at Arianna, whipping my body around. I'm so off-balance I fall over, tripping over the cop's boot as Arianna's being turned around by Officer Richter.

"Don't say anything!" I wrench my head around, craning my neck as I lie awkwardly on the floor with the cuffs tight on my wrists, the cold metal digging into my flesh and shooting sparks of pain up my shoulder, begging her to look at me as I scream out, "Arianna!"

"Take 'em both," Officer Richter tells the other cops.

I stare at Arianna's back, watching as they cuff her.

"Don't touch her!" I scream out so loudly my throat hurts. "She didn't do it!" I shout at them.

"If I were you, I'd wait for your lawyer," Officer Richter tells me as one of the cops ushers her away. My heart is beating so loudly. The sound is deafening.

"Arianna!" I scream for her as I'm heaved off the floor and shoved against the wall as I try to run to her. "Stop!" I scream out. My face is shoved against the wall, and the harsh crack bruises my cheekbone.

"She didn't do it," I breathe out the words. "Leave her alone!" The sounds of them walking her out of the house mixes with the blood rushing in my ears. "Arianna!" I scream again, but she doesn't answer me. Instead, I'm left with silence. Only the two officers and myself remain, alone in my foyer.

"She confessed to a murder. We have to take her in," Officer Lawson says close to my ear. His breathing is ragged from dragging me up and keeping me still against the wall.

"I'll repeat what I said, Mr. Payne." Officer Richter comes into view. His tall frame hovers over me as he tells me, "You should wait for your lawyer."

"She didn't do it." I look him in the eyes, letting him feel my conviction and the truth in my words. She never should have said anything. What was she thinking? My heart twists with a pain that's indescribable.

"She's hurt," I tell them as the man behind me spreads my legs. "She's—"

"She'll be all right, Mr. Payne."

"She didn't do it," I tell him again. I plead with him to let her go. She can't take the fall for this. I won't let her. "She's not feeling well, and she—"

"It doesn't matter. You need to let the law handle this."

The fight that's been absent since I brought my sweetheart home comes back. I won't fight for myself. I'll take the punishment I deserve. But I won't let them touch her. She's innocent. She's always been innocent.

I look him squarely in the eyes as I tell him, "I need to call my lawyer."

CHAPTER 32

ARIANNA

I rest my head on the interrogation table, letting out a heavy exhale. *I won't tell them anything.* I don't care what they say. Or what they do. I refuse to talk. The table is so cold. It makes me want to sleep. I'm so tired. So exhausted. Anxiety twists my stomach as my heart pounds. I assumed they would lock me up right away, toss me in a cell, and throw away the key. But instead, I've been left in a room. I don't know how much time has passed. There isn't a clock in here. Nothing. I'm just alone.

I resist the urge to look behind me. I know they're on the other side of that one-way mirror, looking in. Watching me. I told them I shot him. I don't know how many times. When they asked me why, the answer was easy. But then they asked questions I couldn't answer. Where I got the gun. Why a man's shoe prints were found at the scene. I went silent. I won't say anything that can implicate him in murder. I'm trapped and alone. I turn my head to the other side, letting the chill calm my heated skin.

All for Zander.

I lift my head, sitting back in the metal chair as I remember the look in his eyes when he laid me on the bed. It touched me in ways I couldn't imagine. Made me feel like I was the most precious thing. Like I was *his*.

A tear threatens to fall down my cheek, but I fight it back. I can't break down. Not here. Not *now*.

There's no way I can let Zander take the fall for me. Danny is dead because of me. He killed him to save me. I'm not going to let Zander pay for my mistake. Just the thought of him going to prison for the rest of his life fills me with so much guilt and shame.

No matter what they do or say, I can't let them break me. I pick at my nails, wishing for some miracle, hoping that telling them what he did to me is enough. *It should be*. Shouldn't it?

I keep my neck stiff, staring straight ahead when the door to the interrogation room opens and booted feet smack across this floor. I even keep my head down as the two hardened detectives sit down at the table across from me.

"Are you ready to speak with us, Miss Owens?" Detective Richter asks harshly, a thirty-something tall man with a chiseled jawline and a receding hairline, his deep voice filling the small, hollow room like a bass. Out of the side of my eye, I can see him staring at me with an irritated scowl, his muscular arms folded across his chest. Dressed in a plain white dress shirt and blue jeans, he's not wearing a badge, his gun holstered at his waist.

"I already told you I did it."

The two men share a glance before Detective Richter replies, "You need to give us more than that."

I don't say a word.

"You don't have to be afraid to speak," his partner, Detective Lawson, says more gently, resting his elbows on the table and leaning forward with his hands clasped. He seems the more levelheaded of the two, with short, dark hair, broad shoulders, and a large nose. Unlike Detective Richter, he has a badge, a large golden ornament, proudly on display on his right breast. He doesn't have a gun. "You're away from prying ears now and can speak freely." He waits for a moment to see if I'll respond before saying, "We promise you, we're just trying to do our best to help you."

I nearly snort out a laugh at the bullshit. Though I'm not well-versed in law or cop tactics, I at least know that they are not my friends and they are not trying to help. I would be a fool to trust them.

I keep my head down, clenching my jaw. If they're expecting they'll get me to talk, they'll be waiting a damn long time. I'm not saying shit other than what I've already told them.

The sound of the clock ticking on the wall fills the silence. *Tick tock, tick tock.*

"Look up when Detective Lawson is speaking to you," Detective Richter says irritably.

Go fuck yourself, I want to growl, but I don't.

I know Detective Richter is only doing his job, but he has no idea what I've been through. And if he thinks being firm with me will get him what he wants, then he's sadly mistaken.

"Don't make this hard on yourself. We all know you're lying."

I freeze, wondering if they really do. I almost part my lips to say, "How?" but then remember the tactics the cops use. No matter what they say to me, I need to stay quiet. It's better that way. I'll be quiet. I'll get a lawyer. They can blame me for killing him when they see what he did to me. I'll claim self-defense, or maybe insanity. I pick at my nails, the fear and anxiety weighing heavily against my heart.

"Do you honestly expect us to believe a woman like you killed Danny Brooks when he had so many enemies?" Detective Richter demands.

I remain silent.

Detective Richter snorts when he sees I don't react. "Or let me put it better for you—do you honestly expect us to believe that a woman in your condition, a woman who'd just been beaten within the inch of her life, was in any position to kill her lover?"

Again, I don't respond, keeping my face stoic and pointed downward against the table, even though the word *lover* throws me off.

Just a little while longer, I tell myself.

"You're making this hard for yourself," Detective Lawson says in a way more calming tone. "We don't want to see you locked up for a crime you didn't do. All you have to do is tell us why your new boyfriend killed him."

I stay still, clenching my jaw, my eyes closed tightly.

Silence descends upon the room.

Detective Richter starts to say something, but he's interrupted by a knock at the door.

A young man sticks his head in, opening the door just enough and says, "Someone's here to see you, Detective Richter."

Detective Richter glances at me, his jaw clenching. "Can it wait?"

The man glances outside the door and then shakes his head.

Detective Richter sighs and gets up from his seat and nods to Detective Lawson before leaving the room.

It's quiet when he's gone and I stay in the same position, feeling sharp pricks along my back. I shudder at the thought of having to sleep on a hard bed with my aching wounds.

"Don't be unnerved by Richter," Detective Lawson says, breaking the silence. "He tries to get a rise out of all our interviewees to put them off guard."

I ignore him. He can try to be nice all he wants, but he's not getting anything out of me.

"You can talk to me," Detective Lawson presses. "I'm on your side here."

I continue to sit there, not saying a word. I just want this all to end.

Detective Lawson inhales as if to say more when the door opens and in walks Detective Richter with an impeccably dressed woman in a business suit, her shiny blonde hair finely coiffed.

"Up, Miss Owens," Richter practically barks.

For the first time since coming into the interrogation room, I lift my head, wondering what the hell is going on.

"Why?" I demand, my voice sounding hoarse and raw from screaming the other night. "Is it time for me to go to jail?"

Before he can answer, the woman next to him says, "Hello, Miss Owens. I'm Dana Mills, the lawyer hired to represent you."

"What?" I ask, my face twisting in confusion. "I didn't hire—"

"Mr. Payne hired me as your counsel," Dana says.

I try to keep my hands from trembling. "I'm guilty. I've already admitted that I'm the one who killed Danny Brooks. I'm going to jail."

Dana has a sad expression on her face as she gazes at me, but it quickly turns professional once again. "Please come with me. We've got to get you prepared for your pretrial hearing."

CHAPTER 33

ZANDER

My hands are white-knuckled as I grip onto the back of the wooden row of seats in front of me. This isn't real. It can't be. This isn't how it's supposed to go down.

"Just stay quiet," my father says from my right, and it's a damn good thing my grasp is on the bench. The need to beat the shit out of him is riding me hard. He got me out. He pulled his strings and got me out. *But she's still in custody.*

"She didn't do it," I tell him again. My voice is raw, my eyes stinging and bloodshot. I haven't slept, eaten. I look and feel the same.

"Get yourself together," my father says through clenched teeth as if anyone in here could hear him.

There's hardly a soul in the courtroom. The judge isn't here yet, but the defense, Miss Mills, and prosecution are at their benches as is the court reporter and a few people occupying several seats of the benches where my father and I are. Although we're alone in the row.

"She didn't do it," I tell him again, this time turning my head to face him. He's clean-shaven and his suit is crisp. If anything, he looks better today than he has in years. I'm slumped forward, and next to him, I imagine I look the opposite. Unkempt, although my suit is at least clean and pressed.

I let out a shaky breath as the back door opens in front of me, just to the left of the witness stand, and a cop ushers my sweetheart in.

My heart crumples in my chest as I lean forward. She doesn't look at me. Her eyes are on her hands as she walks in.

I hate my father. I hate trusting him. He promised me she'd be all right. But this is too much.

Please don't say anything, Arianna.

They couldn't charge me with her confession. My father's spinning stories in the press and coming up with plans and deals. But all of them leave her here in the courtroom to face the charges. I only need to hear the bail amount so I can pay it and take her away.

We can run. I'll run forever with her. I have enough money. I'll take her wherever we can hide.

"All rise," the bailiff says in a commanding voice, and I lift my heavy body, but I don't move my eyes away from my sweetheart.

Her hair sways as she stands, and I get a glimpse of her

profile as she turns her head to watch the judge come through the heavy double doors on the right. Her cheeks are reddened and tearstained. The sight of her in an orange jumpsuit shreds me.

My father's hand rests on my shoulder, and I slowly pull my eyes away from her to look into his gaze. The same eyes as mine.

"She'll be fine," he tells me beneath his breath. The bail hearing continues as I search his face for something to give me confidence in him, trying to settle the disdain rising to the surface.

"And what are the allegations against the defendant?" I hear the judge's heavy voice call out.

"Murder in the second degree," the prosecution answers the judge.

"I need her out of here," I tell my father, my body trembling with the need to go to her. The skin over my knuckles feels as though it will split if I grip the bench any harder.

"She shouldn't be there—" I tell him, but he cuts me off.

"Quiet," my father hisses, the admonishment clear in his voice. I've never needed him. Not for one goddamned thing in my life. But right now, I do.

"She's not a flight risk," I hear my attorney say. Dana's the best there is. She'll get her out. But I need it to happen now. Today.

"On the contrary, it's evident that she has access to financial means. Enough to flee the country."

"What access?" Miss Mills asks with disbelief. The room spins around me as I take in the words, white noise drowning out parts of the conversation as I turn back to Arianna. She's staring ahead just as she was on the stage at the auction. *Accepting her fate.*

"She's involved with an individual with enough money and means, and reason, might I add, to carry her out of the country." My heart sinks in my chest. No. No. They can't keep her.

"The charges against my client make it clear that no one else is in danger of—" my attorney rebuts.

"She confessed to murder," the prosecution cuts off my attorney.

"What was said is inadmissible. She was under duress at the time and the prosecution is well aware of the circumstances."

"I did it!" The words are ripped from my throat as I stand there, staring at the judge. I can feel her eyes on me as I step out into the aisle, finally letting go of the bench.

My father reaches for me, grabbing my arm and shoving his hand over my mouth. I turn in his grasp and land my fist against his jaw, the stinging pain ringing through my numb body.

"Zander," my father looks back at me with his hand over his jaw. There's a bit of blood covering his teeth and spilling out onto his hand. His face isn't one of anger. There's no hate. His expression is simply one of denial.

"I shot Daniel Brooks twice." I turn and face the judge,

only then aware of the sounds of the people around me and the flash of a camera.

"Zander, no!" Arianna's soft voice travels to me, her words full of pain. I close my eyes, ignoring her plea. She never should have tried to pull this shit. I won't let her. I swallow thickly and continue.

"I came to his home and saw the defendant there. I knew she was there." My father tries to cut me off, but I continue. "I came with my gun and I shot him." The words leave my hollow chest, each one ripping and clawing at my throat on the way out, begging to take the memories with them. "I killed him, and I'd do it again."

"This is a stunt, Your Honor," the prosecution calls out, his voice high and carrying an air of disbelief.

I catch sight of my attorney, but she's looking at my father, her lips pressed together.

Through all the banging of the gavel, the chatter of the people behind me, the attorneys arguing, and the judge speaking over everyone, all I can hear is Arianna. "Zander, no," and her small cry breaks my heart.

I hear the footsteps of the cop's shoes against the thin carpet of the courtroom before his hands are on me.

CHAPTER 34

ARIANNA

"You're a free woman, Miss Owens," Dana tells me as we pull up to my shared apartment with Natalie, the smooth hum of the Mercedes engine running.

Her words bring me no joy. I don't want to be free. I shouldn't be here.

I suck in a sharp breath as Zander's words ring in my mind. *I did it! I shot Daniel Brooks twice.*

I shake my head at the memory, filled with despair. He should've kept quiet. He should've let me take the fall.

Seeing him dragged from the courtroom nearly brought me to my knees.

Noting the anguish on my face, Dana gently pats me on the knee. "That's a brave thing you did, trying to take the fall for Mr. Payne."

I make a face. "Brave? Or stupid?" The question is

rhetorical. What I did wasn't smart, but smart doesn't matter in this case.

A wistful, empathetic expression comes over Dana. "I think we've all done something not so wise in the name of love, Miss Owens."

I inhale deeply at the word *love*. It's true. And something I've known for a while now. I love Zander. And I don't want to see him rot in a jail cell on my behalf no matter what he did.

"Don't worry," Dana assures me at my distant, pained expression. "Everything is going to work out fine."

"Do you think so?" I ask, feeling a small glimmer of hope.

Dana gives me a confident nod. "Mr. Payne is a resourceful man. And so is his father. If anyone can figure a way out of this mess, they can."

I know she's trying to comfort me, but she can't know that for sure. Zander committed murder. Even confessed to it. I want to believe that things are going to be okay, but right now, I'm not seeing a way out.

"Thank you," I say to Dana, giving a nod and flashing a weak smile. "I really appreciate all of your help."

"You're very welcome, Miss Owens," Dana replies. "Take care."

I open the door and step out of the vehicle and watch as she drives off in her gleaming chrome Mercedes-Benz. After a moment, I turn around and take in the apartment building, noting the cream-colored stucco walls and the units that are almost too close together.

It feels strange coming back here after everything I've gone through. And I dread having to go inside, knowing the questions that await me there. But I have to do it. I need someone to confide in.

My heart races as I make my way up the stairs and to my apartment with Natalie. By the time I reach the door, my breathing is heavy and ragged, a little from climbing the stairs and some from the crushing anxiety that I feel.

"What the hell is going on, Ari?" Natalie demands as soon as I step through the door.

My chest fills with warmth at the sight of her. I haven't seen her in days and I'm grateful to finally lay eyes on her face. She looks beside herself, her hair's a mess, and it looks like she's lost a few pounds in the little time since I last saw her.

"Your mug has been plastered all over the news!" Natalie hisses when I don't answer right away. "It's crazy!" She shakes her head in anger. "I tried getting into the courthouse to see you, but I couldn't get inside." She pauses, peering at me with concern. "Is it really true?"

"Is what true?" I ask.

"Did that Zander . . . Zander Payne . . . did he really murder Danny to save you?" Natalie asks with intensity.

I stare at her for a long time, setting my keys down on the

counter and recounting the last few weeks. It hurts to take in a breath as I look back at her wide, pleading eyes. Slowly, I nod my head. "He did . . . if he hadn't . . ." my voice trails off as pain pulses my back. My wounds have been healing, but they still hurt like hell. I don't know when the pain will stop. If it will *ever* stop. I'll have scars for the rest of my life, but none of that matters compared to what Zander's facing.

"Jesus," Natalie mutters, shaking her head. "I can't believe it." She looks up at me, her eyes shining with relief. "Thank God you're still alive." She comes forward to give me a hug.

I hold her at arm's length. "Please don't touch me."

She covers her mouth quickly, pain reflected in her eyes. "I'm sorry," she breathes the words. She visibly swallows as I lower my arms. "He hit you, right? Danny did?" Her words are slow, said with a lowered voice.

I turn around and lift my shirt slightly up my back for a moment. Natalie recoils as I turn back around, her face twisting in disgusted disbelief.

Silence falls over the room for a moment.

"I need you to tell me everything," Natalie says, finally breaking the silence. She looks shaken to the core, visibly trembling.

"I don't want to talk, Nat." My voice is soft. I don't want to do anything except wait for Zander to be released. Tears leak from the corners of my eyes. He can't go to jail for me for the rest of my life. I don't think I could live with the guilt.

"Please, Ari?" she asks as I brush the tears away. "I've

been worried sick about you since this all started. I don't think I can go another minute without knowing what happened." She shakes her head, tears filling her eyes. "Not after" —she pauses and swallows thickly— "seeing that."

I suck in a trembling breath, more tears threatening to spill from my eyes. The pain in Natalie's voice causes my knees to go weak, and I feel like crumpling to the floor. I stumble over to the couch and sink down into the cushions, wanting to curl up into a tiny ball. Crossing my arms across my chest, I bite my lower lip and lower my head. The shame, guilt, and anxiety are almost too much for me to take.

I've been a shitty friend, keeping secrets and leaving Natalie in the dark.

A moment later, I feel the space beside me dip as Natalie takes a seat and a warm hand gently touches my shoulder.

"Please don't do this," Natalie begs, her heart in her voice. "Please don't push me away right now."

The pain in her words lances my chest.

"Ari?" she presses. "Please. My heart is aching."

When I can manage over the lump in my throat, I tell her, "I'm so, so sorry for keeping things from you. I never meant to hurt you."

"Oh, honey," Natalie says, her voice filled with unshed tears, aching with sympathy. "You don't have to be sorry for me. I'll be fine. I'm just happy that you're okay."

I try to respond, but I can't get any words out.

Natalie keeps rubbing my shoulders until I'm all cried out, softly whispering soothing comfort in my ears. "Can you forgive me?" I ask hoarsely when I finally recover, looking at her with red-rimmed eyes. Natalie grabs a tissue from the end table and dabs at the tears on my face. "Oh, Ari . . . there's nothing to forgive. I love you and am here for you no matter what."

Her words are almost enough to send me into another bout of tears, but I swallow them back.

"I just need to know what happened," Natalie says softly.

I stare at her long and hard. Her eyes are puffy and swollen. I didn't notice it when I came through the door.

Sucking in a deep, trembling breath, I tell her everything. About Danny and his abusive, manipulative ways, his debts, him owing Zander and using me as collateral for the auction, and Zander's confession. *Everything.*

"Shit, Ari," Natalie whispers when I'm done, her eyes filled with tears and horror as she shakes her head. "I never knew."

"It's awful," I say weakly.

There's pain in Natalie's face. And it's hard for me not to avert my gaze. "Why didn't you tell me?"

I pick nervously at my blouse. "I don't know. I felt like . . . I was trapped. The club, it has NDAs. I'm not supposed to talk to other people about it unless I've been permitted."

"You could've still told me," Natalie said, looking hurt. "I would've never told anyone."

I let out a distressed sigh. "I know, Nat. I just didn't know what to do and I didn't want to disappoint you. I'm sorry. "Nat grabs my hand and squeezes it. "Don't be." She gives my hand another gentle squeeze. "I'm just glad you're alive."

I close my eyes, remembering the brutal lashes Danny gave me and whisper, "Me, too."

"And I'm glad that bastard Danny is dead," Natalie says with venom as though my thoughts summoned him to her mind.

I part my lips out of habit to defend him but then close them. For the first time I can remember, I have no urge to come to Danny's defense. It used to come so easily to me, like a reflex, but now I owe him nothing.

"I'm glad he's gone too," I agree, and I mean it.

There's a moment of silence and I can only hear the sound of my heartbeat.

"So, what happens now?" Natalie asks. "What's going to happen to Zander?"

It's the question that's been on my mind since the moment I saw him dragged out of the courtroom. I like to believe with all his money and power, Zander could somehow find a way out of this. He's too smart, charming, and cunning to let himself be locked away for the rest of his life.

But deep down, I know his chances are slim. He

confessed. They have all the evidence they need to put him away. And no amount of money he has is going to save him.

A heavy sigh escapes my lips and I grip Natalie's hand tightly as I reply, "I really hope so, Nat. I really do."

CHAPTER 35

ZANDER

One slip, and your world crumbles around you. My elbows rest on my knees in the large cell. The holding area is quiet, the only sounds coming from a vent above my head and occasionally a door opening or closing. I lift my head to stare at the steel bars.

I'm fucked. I take in a deep breath, exhaustion weighing me down. There's nothing I can do or say to protect myself. Judgment day has come. I let out a shaky laugh that echoes off the empty walls.

How ironic. All the shitty things I've done, the laws I've broken and corrupt deals I've made, and yet I'm going to be sentenced for the one good thing I ever did.

The smile fades as I see the look in Arianna's eyes. The fear. The realization of what was happening.

I run my hands through my hair, my eyes glassing with tears. The hardest thing is walking away from her. *My sweetheart.*

It's only been hours since the hearing. Hours since they cuffed me and took me here.

I was silent in the interrogation room. I'm smart enough to shut up when I'm alone.

A long sigh leaves me as I slump against the cold brick wall, staring aimlessly ahead. It's odd how much relief I feel now that it's all over. No more deals and corruption, no more hiding in the shadows and watching but smiling when the lights are on me. No more pretending and playing their game.

Even if I somehow get out of here, I'm done. I'm through with all of this shit.

I want more from life. I want a real life. One with Arianna.

Women make men fall to their knees

I wouldn't change a thing. But now I'm not there for her.

I close my eyes slowly, picturing her sweet smile. Genuine happiness. She gave that to me, and I'll be damned, but I want more.

My eyes open and the vision of her disappears. If only I could go back and somehow hide it. No. I'd need to go back to before. To when he gave her to me. I'd go back then if I could and hire Charles to end him.

I should have. I made so many mistakes, tripping and stumbling, and all the while, my eyes were only on Arianna.

She made me fall, and now I only want to get up for her.

The sound of the large door at the end of the hall opening snaps me back to the moment.

Several sets of shoes slap against the hard floor as they make their way closer to me.

I stay still, my heart beating slowly and my blood chilling. I know how this all ends, but I can't help to wish for an out. Someone who owes me, someone I've helped in the past who can pull strings. But there's not a single name I can think of. None connected to Judge Pierce. And I've confessed in a room of eyes and ears.

I should have played this smarter, but I couldn't think. Not with her taking the fall for me.

The warden doesn't look at me as he slips a key into the lock, opening the large cell door by pulling on the first bar. Behind him are two men.

The first I recognize as my father's lawyer. Not my own. Nathanael Goldman.

My father's behind him. Immediately, I stand, rising to meet them. The warden closes the door behind them as anxiety races in my blood. I can hardly look my father in the eyes, but somehow I do. I may have killed Brooks, but he deserved to die.

"I know you didn't do it." My father's voice is full of pride and confidence.

"I did." I look him in the eyes as I answer. My father's

jaw clenches and he looks to his right, to the lawyer he's brought with him.

"I didn't hear anything," Goldman answers, leaning against the bricked cell wall, with his eyes focused through the bars and on the door at the end of the hall.

I look back to my father, staring into his eyes that reflect disbelief and something else. Disappointment. Never in my life have I seen him look at me like that. I have to tear my eyes away from him, shame seeping into my blood. My father's done a lot of wrongs in his life.

But I murdered a man.

"He hit her," I say the words, and my bastard emotions come through, making my voice crack. "He beat her so hard, so violently, she couldn't even move. There was so much blood."

"Zander . . ." my father's voice is nearly a whisper.

"I'm sorry, but I don't take it back." My eyes close tight as I sit back on the bench, the image of her on the floor refusing to leave me.

I jump back at the feel of a strong hand on my shoulder. My eyes fly up to meet my father's. His eyes are glazed as he nods his head. "I can understand that."

He starts to sit next to me but stands tall instead, running a hand down his face. "I just . . ." He takes in a deep breath, looking at the wall and lowering his head. "I don't want to believe it," he says in a low voice.

"I couldn't help myself," I tell him as I stare at my hands, feeling the anger pouring out of me as I killed him, stealing the life from him and making sure he'd never strike her again.

"You'll never speak of this." My father turns to face me again, his voice coming in stronger. "Ever. To anyone."

I stare at him, not understanding. "I can't lie on the stand," I tell him.

His brow furrows for a moment, and then he shakes his head before he says, "There won't be a trial."

I'm dumbfounded, still not understanding. "You aren't the only one who didn't like Daniel Brooks. And your Arianna wasn't the first woman he struck." My father shares a look with Goldman before continuing. "If you'd just been quiet, she would have gotten off." Anger flashes in his eyes for a moment as he continues, "If you'd just listened to me and kept quiet—"

I rise from my seat, meeting my father eye to eye. "I couldn't risk her." My voice comes out firm and barely hiding a threat. "I'll never risk her. I won't ever let her pay for my sins."

It's quiet for a long moment. My chest rises and falls with sporadic breaths, remembering how she took the fall for me. I wish she hadn't. I wish she'd never said a word.

"It doesn't matter. You're still my son. I'm not letting you sit behind bars."

"It'll be out in the papers."

My father scoffs. "It's already out!"

I lower my head, my blood heating. My reputation is ruined.

"Payments have been sent," Goldman says softly from the far side of the cell.

"Right, right," my father says, pacing the room. "We can romanticize it?" my father asks Goldman.

The lawyer nods once, his eyes flickering to my father's before turning back to outside the cell.

"So, what's going to happen?" I ask, for the first time feeling as though there's hope.

"You'll be free from charges based on inconsistent evidence. And the papers will paint it as if it's a tragedy and Daniel Brooks was a monster—"

"It's the truth." My voice is hard as I cut him off. "What he did to her . . ." I say, and my hands shake as they clench into fists.

"What's important is the fact that you'll be fine," my father says with a hard edge as he walks to the far wall, the wheels turning in his head. A bit of a breath leaves me, and I nearly fall forward.

"It's done then?" I ask in disbelief.

My father turns sharply toward me and says, "So long as you fucking listen." I stare into his eyes, but I don't see a hint of anger, only fear. I nod my head once, swallowing the lump in my throat. I'm stunned. I've only ever felt a sense of competition between the two of us. But all I have for him in this moment is gratitude. He's sending me back to her. The thought makes me close my eyes, and her beautiful smile comes back to me.

"You love her?" my father asks, taking me by surprise. I don't answer him. I know with everything in me that I do. But a man like him wouldn't understand.

"I loved your mother," he says as if reading my mind.

My father motions toward Goldman.

"Just make sure she loves you back, Zander." My father's voice wavers as he starts to leave the cell.

"She does," I answer him quickly, making him halt in his steps. I may be a fool in many ways. But there's no doubt in my mind that she loves me as much as I love her.

My father turns to look at me, a genuine concern in his eyes.

"I know she does," I tell him before he can say whatever's on his mind. "I know she does," I repeat, and my voice is low, but the conviction is there. I don't need to prove anything to anyone, but for whatever fucked up reason, I need my father to know that she does.

He nods his head once, his eyes on the floor of the cell. His lips part again, but no words come out. He pats his hand against the bars and Goldman gestures to whoever's waiting. The sound of heavy boots coming closer down the cement hall echoes off the walls.

"I hope you're right, Son," my father says in a low voice. A small bit of doubt creeps into the back of my mind.

She's never said the words. And neither have I. She has no idea. She's never known.

"You'll be out within the hour. Just don't say anything," Goldman tells me as the warden opens the cell and the two of them leave me alone. My thoughts are consumed with what will happen to Arianna now that Brooks is dead.

I have a contract to keep her, but she doesn't have to stay.

I'll do anything I can to keep her.

CHAPTER 36

ARIANNA

They look so happy. Standing in the hallway of Zander's estate, I grip the picture frame in my hands, a solo tear rolling down my right cheek. They look like the perfect family. Zander, with his gorgeous smile. And his two parents looking on as if they're so proud of their son.

My heart aches as I stare at the portrait, my eyes on Zander's mother. She's gone now. And if she knew what was going to happen to her son, she'd probably be devastated. Guilt presses down on my chest as another tear rolls down my cheek.

This is all my fault.

I wish I could tell him that I'm sorry. That I didn't mean for any of this to happen. That I wish I could take it all back. I wish I could go back to the very beginning. When all of this started. I wish I'd killed Danny myself.

A huge lump forms in my throat as try to hold back the tide of tears that threatens to fall from my eyes.

The guilt is almost enough to choke on.

It wasn't supposed to end up this way.

I squeeze the picture frame against my chest, despair and anger coursing through me.

"You okay, sweetheart?" asks a deep, sexy voice.

I look up and cover my mouth with my hand, nearly collapsing on the floor.

"Zander!" I cry, setting down the picture frame on the oak wood stand with shaky hands. It falls over, but I don't care. I have to run to him. To feel him. I bury my face into his chest and hold him with everything I have in me. *I'll never let him go.*

"How did you . . ." my voice trails off as I'm at a loss for words when I lean back to look at him.

He smiles weakly down at me, his eyes focusing on a stray strand of hair in my face as he brushes it away and leans forward to kiss me. The simple touch melts me. My body relaxes into him, finally feeling the warmth of his body. "I'm not going to be charged."

His words hit me slowly, taking their time before I fully comprehend what he's saying. I pull away from him out of shock, but he holds my lower waist close to him as I stare into his eyes.

I can't speak. My voice is robbed from me from the shock. I shake my head slightly and ask, "No charges?"

"Nothing."

"How?" I finally manage softly.

Zander's eyes go dark momentarily, his body tensing. "My father has his connections," he replies, his voice low. "He's still owed a lot of favors."

"Is everything . . ." I breathe when I get over my shock. "Is everything okay? It's over?"

I can barely breathe as he pulls me into his chest. His hand is gentle on my back, but still it stings to the touch. "Sorry," he breathes into my hair as I settle against his chest. I don't give a fuck about my back. Not right now. I bury my face into his shirt, just breathing him in. "It's all over."

I don't want to let go.

I'm afraid if I do, I'll lose him forever. And I'll never have a chance to hold him again.

"I've got you," Zander whispers as he kisses my hair. "And I'm not letting you go."

I close my eyes and nestle deeper into him. *Don't. Please don't ever let me go.* "There's something I've been wanting to let you know for a while now. Something that I've wanted to say but haven't had the courage." I talk with my eyes closed, but he pulls back to look into my face and I have to stare into his eyes to tell him.

Zander arches an eyebrow with curiosity. "What's that?"

A large lump forms in my throat.

"I love you, Zander Payne," I tell him, my voice aching with emotion.

Zander doesn't respond immediately, causing my heart to skip as I wait for his response. It's beating so fast and hard I'm sure he can feel it pumping against his chest. But when he breaks out into a handsome grin, I know I have nothing to worry about.

"And I love you too, Arianna Owens," Zander says softly, coming in for a deep, passionate kiss. "And I always will."

EPILOGUE

ZANDER

"They'll be expecting you." My father's voice comes out clearly on the phone.

"I understand that," I answer him simply, walking out of the kitchen with the phone to my ear. It's the *Gala of the Year*, the third one with that title so far.

Veronica Marsett is hosting it for her charity, and over four hundred attendees will be there. Most of whom I know firsthand, and half of them will be expecting me to address them. To notice them publicly and pose for photo ops. To rub elbows, as my father used to say when I was younger.

These are the scenes that matter most. It's all about who you're seen with.

But with my Arianna, my sweetheart hardly sleeping, I doubt she's going to want to go. And if she's not with me, I'm not going.

I don't want to be anywhere without her by my side.

Because my father's right. It's all about who you're seen with. That's who matters. And right now, she's the only one who matters to me.

Even if he saved me. He can wait. Business will always wait from now on.

"You're really going to snub them?" Oddly enough, my father's voice holds only a trace of admonishment.

"It's not a snub. She's not feeling well."

My father's silent on the phone for a moment. The glow from the fire in the back of the library lights the dim room. The floor-to-ceiling curtains are closed tight on the far end, but the ones closest to me are open, just enough for someone to peek through.

I keep the phone to my ear as I peek out and see the snow settling on the ground. Early February has brought enough snow to lock us in for weeks, but I'm fine with that.

I turn around to face the large leather sofa as my father starts talking. It groans as Arianna shifts her weight on it to get comfortable. Her hand rests on her swollen belly, but she's sleeping soundly.

I hate that she can't fall asleep in bed with me. I guess I'll have to start sleeping out here.

"There are deals to finalize, and if you're seen with the right investors, that will make their bids rise." He tells me things I already know, but I simply don't care anymore. There's so much more than money. More than power. There's love.

Arianna's belly rises with a deep breath as she slowly rolls onto her side, dragging a cream chenille throw with her as she goes.

There's a feeling of being complete. Of not wanting anything more than what you already have.

A soft sigh of satisfaction falls from her sweet lips.

"I'm sure they'll understand," I speak softly into the phone, but Arianna's eyes flutter open. A small smile spreads on her face when she sees me.

It's a genuine smile, one that makes me reciprocate.

My feet move of their own accord, drawn to her. I crouch down to the floor beside her and plant a kiss on the tip of her nose.

"I have to go," I tell my father, cutting off whatever reason he's trying to convince me of to go.

"Wait!" I'm surprised from my father's sharp voice. It takes me aback and I flinch, pulling the phone away slightly.

Arianna rises on her elbow, wiping the sleep from her eyes and staring at the phone. She's not used to my father's temper, and to be honest, it's been a long time since I've had to deal with it. I won't let her witness this. I rise to my feet, straightening my shoulders and preparing to tell my father off.

He's been agitated lately with me leaving more and more work in his hands, or simply letting go. There are plenty of investors, and I'm not interested in certain deals anymore. Not when I have so much to protect now.

My lips part as I suck in a breath, prepared for the worst, but I wasn't anticipating the words that come from the other end of the phone.

"The baby shower—that's next month?" my father asks me, clearing his throat and waiting for a response.

A deep crease settles in my forehead as I turn back to look at Arianna over my shoulder.

"It's next month, yes." I wait for a moment, still feeling tense and on edge as Arianna stands up, holding her stomach as though it will fall if she lets go. She's so beautiful, carrying my child. There's been a glow about her since she found out.

"I'd like to go," my father says with firm conviction.

"It's not for men," I say, and the words spill out of my mouth with disbelief.

"Sure it is. We'll go at the end. Your mother loved that." I'm taken aback by his confession. "You go at the end with a gift for her and help load all the things. It's what you do," he says matter-of-factly. "It's probably the last thing I did right with your mother. But I know it's a good thing to do . . . and I want to help you."

My body's frozen in place as Arianna walks toward me, one hand rubbing soothing circles over her swollen bump and the other bracing a hand on her back.

"Sure," I answer my father. The vision of what he

must've looked like back then plays in my mind. Maybe they were happy then, all those years ago.

"It's settled then. I'm sure I'll see you before then?" The words come out as a question.

"Sure," I say again, wrapping an arm around Arianna's waist as she leans into me, her eyes wide with questions but her body relaxed.

"Very well then. I'll talk to you soon." There's a silence between us for a moment, and for the first time in years, I feel the urge to tell him I love him. As though it's real, but I don't. Maybe another time. The line goes dead, and I pull the phone away from my ear to stare at it in my hand.

"Are you all right?" she asks, and her voice is soft, tinged with concern.

I toss the phone down onto the sofa a few feet away and turn her in my arms. Her belly rubs against mine as I pull her in close. "Of course."

She eyes me warily, her one eyebrow lifting with skepticism.

"Everything is wonderful."

That sweet smile plays at her lips again, and she nods as she says, "It is, isn't it?"

I kiss her lips softly, but she deepens it. My greedy sweetheart. I'm more than happy to give her more. I'd hand her over the world in exchange for what she's given me.

When she breaks the kiss, I whisper between us, "I love you."

"I love you too, Zander."

Don't stop reading!

If you loved Given, you'll devour Forsaken. Turn the page for a sneak peek!

If you haven't read all the highest bidder series, keep turning the pages for a sneak peek of the first in the series, Bought, Lucian's story, available now!

Want more? Join our mailing list to receive bonus deleted scenes! (If you're already on our lists, you'll get this automatically).

BOUGHT: HIGHEST BIDDER

BOOK 1 OF THE HIGHEST BIDDER SERIES

Prologue

Lucian

I slowly pace the room, letting the sound of my shoes clacking against the floor startle her. My eyes are on Dahlia, watching her every movement. Her breathing picks up as she realizes I've come back for her. With her blindfold on and her wrists and ankles tied to the bed while she lies on her belly, she's at my complete mercy, and she knows it.

The sight of her bound and waiting for me is so tempting. I force my groan back.

Her pale, milky skin is on full display as she waits for me. I've left her like this deliberately, in this specific position. She knows now not to move, not to struggle. She knows to wait for me obediently, and what's more, *she enjoys it*.

The wooden paddle gently grazes along her skin, leaving goosebumps down her thigh in its wake. They trail up the curve of her ass, and her shoulders rise as she sucks in a breath. Her body tenses and her lips part, spilling a soft moan. She knows what's coming.

She's *earned* this.

She lied to me.

And she's going to be punished.

She doesn't know this is for her own good. She should, but she hasn't realized it yet.

I'm only doing this for her. She *needs* this.

She needs to heal, and I know just how to help her. The paddle whips through the air and smacks her lush ass, leaving a bright red mark as she gasps, her hands gripping the binds at her wrists. I watch as her pussy clenches around nothing, making my dick that much harder.

Soon.

I barely maintain my control and gently knead her ass, soothing the pulsing pain I know she's feeling. "Tell me why you lied to me, treasure," I whisper at the shell of her ear, my lips barely touching her sensitive skin.

"I'm sorry," she whimpers with lust. I don't want her apology. I want her to realize what she's done. I want to know why she hid it from me all this time. She'll learn she can't lie to me. There's no reason she should.

Smack! I bring the paddle down on the other cheek and

her body jolts as a strangled cry leaves her lips, her pussy glistening with arousal.

"That's not what I asked, treasure." My tone is taunting. She needs to realize what I already know. She needs to admit it. To me, but mostly to herself.

I pull away from her, just for a moment, leaving her to writhe on the bed from the sting of the paddle.

I didn't anticipate our relationship reaching this point.

In the beginning, I thought this would be fun. Just a form of stress relief for me.

But things changed.

I bought her at auction, and now she can't leave. She's mine for an entire month. But the days have flown by, and the contract is almost over.

I need more time.

I'm going to make this right. I'm going to heal my treasure.

If it's the last thing I do, I'll give her what she needs. What we both need.

She parts those beautiful lips, and hope blooms in my chest.

Say it, tell me what you desperately need to say.

But her mouth closes, and she shifts slightly on the sheets before stilling and waiting patiently for more.

I pull my arm back and steady myself. Soon, she'll

realize it. My broken treasure. Soon she'll be *healed*, but that won't be enough for me anymore. I want more.

Smack!

Click here to keep reading Bought!

SNEAK PEEK OF FORSAKEN

Grace

Beaten. Broken. Used as a bargaining chip. I've been through hell. *He* can't do anything that hasn't already been done to me. Except show me tenderness, kindness... pleasure. And he has. In a way I didn't know I needed.

Goosebumps travel down my arms as I hear his heavy footsteps echoing in the hall. My steady heartbeat quickens.

He's come back for me. I'm almost surprised by the excitement I feel. The rush of adrenaline, and the anticipation of hearing the click of the lock on the door. *Almost.*

My fingers wrap around the thin bars as he enters. My captor. I could come out, I could let him have me. I know Gio wants me, and I'd be a liar if I said I didn't want him, too. His hard ripped body and the heat in his eyes tempt me to come out of my cage. The door's never locked, so I could easily leave. But I'm safe here.

He said he won't touch me, and he's held firm to his promise. So long as I stay inside of the cage, I'm protected. But I want to come out. I want his praise. *I've grown addicted to it*. His very presence is a drug.

I'm desperate for him, and he knows it. I want to resist. I want to hold out against whatever sickness is taking me over. But I can't. He's too much. *He's everything*.

There's a darkness inside of him, a dangerous beast. I know what he's capable of, but when he's with me, there's a sense of calm about him. Maybe I'm naive to think I affect him as much as he does me, but the very thought that I do makes me feel powerful.

The sound of the door creaking open and his broad shoulders filling up the doorway make my lips part, and a moan of lust escapes my throat. My nipples harden, and my clit throbs with need. He's done this to me. He's trained me to react like this. I know it's the truth, but I can't deny I enjoy it.

"My princess," he says and his voice is rough and deep. It reminds me of how he groaned when he first took me. It's the sexiest fucking sound I've ever heard. He's just as obsessed with me as I am with him. It's only fair.

I lick my lips and shift on my knees, facing him and leaning forward. I don't leave the safety of the cage though. I want him to lure me out. Is that so wrong?

"I miss you," he whispers, crouching in front of the cage, his fingers curling above mine around the bars. My heart thumps hard in my chest, and my body begs me to just reach out. To climb into his lap and let him hold me. It's my choice. But the only choice I've been given.

I've never felt so loved before. Even if it's an illusion and nothing more.

But that doesn't stop me from craving it.

"Tell me you missed me," e commands, and my mouth parts on its own. The words are there, right on the tip of my tongue. I flirt with the idea of saying them, but I close my lips shut tight

He tilts his head, narrowing his eyes and tsking me for disobeying him. Again I shift on my knees, questioning my decision to keep fighting him.

His expression softens as he sits in front of me, lowering himself as my eyes look down at him. I settle onto the floor of the cage across from him. Merely inches away, but so much farther than that all the same.

"I know you did." As he says the words, his dark eyes heat and a cocky grin plays at his lips.

I can't help my eyes widening and a smile slowly slipping across my lips. I wish I could hide it, but I can't hide anything from him. Not anymore.

I don't want to go back to the way things were. I know it's wrong, but I had nothing before him. I'm drunk on his touch, his words. He's everything I could possibly need. He's shown me that.

I may be broken. But I'm *his*.

Gio
One month before

THE BRIGHT RED RUBBER BALL SQUEAKS AS I RELEASE IT, watching it sail far across my yard. Duke, my loyal black lab, turns and chases the ball as fast as he can, tearing up the grass in pursuit.

I smile to myself, looking out across the property. I like the seclusion and privacy of living outside of the city, and I was able to construct a home with everything I could need. I bought the place more for the land than for anything else. I'd be happy living in a fucking trailer if it meant I could do whatever I damn well please, but fortunately I get paid a lot of money to do what I do.

"You know we can't turn this down."

I glance at my father at the sound of his voice. He stands impatiently against a nearby tree, puffing one of the short, dark cigars he prefers. His receding white hair makes him look ten years older than he is. He's wearing his usual outfit, a blue dress shirt tucked into jeans with a brown work jacket over top and oversized brown boots that are nearly falling apart. He looks like a construction worker, or something blue collar like that.

He sure as hell works with his hands, but he's no fucking construction worker.

"You know that if we do it, the consequences could be

extensive," I answer, feeling a chill run down my shoulders.

Duke grabs the ball and heads back, his tail held high in the air. My father huffs, shaking his head and then inhales deeply, looking past me.

His voice is low as he responds, "I understand your concerns, but this is beyond us."

"Exactly. It's too big to control," I answer, not bothering to look at him.

"Control?" He laughs. "There's no control in our line of work."

"Maybe the way you operate. But that's not how I do things."

He pushes off the tree and walks toward me just as Duke drops the ball at my feet. I pick it up and launch it again, sending the dog running. The smell of the cigar gets stronger as he walks closer.

"Listen, son. You know how much this means to me."

Guilt threatens to take over. The only man I owe shit to is my father. But he's falling for a trap. They'll never give him what he wants. "I know what it *could* mean, at least."

"We've been outsiders our whole fucking lives." His voice rises, letting his emotions come through.

"I know," I say, jaw tense.

"They think we're garbage and trash," he says, nearly

spitting the words. "But this is our chance to show them that we're dependable. That we belong."

I grunt and watch the dog sprint off in the distance. My father's right, even though his motives are pretty fucking skewed. He's lived his entire life on the outskirts of the Romano *familia*, wishing he could be a part of them, but unable to join. He's only half Italian; his disgraced father ran off and fucked some Irish girl years and years ago. It doesn't matter to me, but my father never got over the fact that his full Italian Romano cousins were allowed into the *familia*, while he was kept at a distance.

That's probably why my father entered into this profession and trained me to work alongside him. Being hitmen means we're allowed to exist on the fringe of the *familia*. We've even earned some respect, though fear may be the better word for it. Over the years my father gathered a particular set of skills and passed them down to me, continuing the family tradition.

I don't give a shit about my inbred, shitheel cousins. I could kill them one by one if I wanted and never lose a wink of sleep. Blood means nothing to me.

I don't give a fuck about the *familia* like my father does. He has this chip on his shoulder and acts like all of our problems are due to the *familia* rejecting him. He can't see past his own petty need to be accepted by them.

Being an outsider suits me. I like my life outside of the city, and outside of the *familia*. I take their money and do their jobs because that's the life I know, but I don't want to be a part of their politics and their bullshit.

Taking this job offer though would destroy any

semblance of outsider status and shove us right into the high-stakes world of mafia power plays. I don't fucking want that. I'm not interested.

"Think of the money," he tries to persuade me. "I know you don't care about the *familia* like I do." There's a hint of bitterness in his tone, and it makes my body tense. "But think of the money they're offering."

He has a good point. They're offering to pay us triple our normal rate, which is significant already. The target is difficult to get to and very important, but the money is absurdly good.

A man could possibly retire with that kind of cash.

"If we do this, our lives will change," I say, meeting his cold gaze.

"Exactly." My father smiles, his yellowed teeth showing for only a moment before he takes another puff of his cigar.

I shake my head. "You see it as a good thing, but to me this would destroy everything we've built."

His boots are heavy and his steps quick as he tosses the cigar aside. He walks up to me and suddenly grabs my jacket by the collar, bunching the fabric up in his fists. My hands clench into fists, but I wait. I'm used to this. I grew up with it.

I can see the anger in his eyes, the intense fury that dwells deep inside. It's a darkness that eats away at him, and I know that he drinks more than he should to try and keep it at bay.

I have the same darkness inside of me. It comes out in different ways, but it's there, slowly rotting me from the inside. I hate my father in this moment because I see myself in him, and it disgusts me. My knuckles go white and adrenaline pumps hard in my blood, but I keep it down, waiting for him to get out whatever's on his mind.

He better do it quick, 'cause I don't have time for this shit.

"You can't fuck this up for me," he growls. His face is close to mine, but I don't move. I don't give him the opportunity to see me weak. "The *familia*'s denied me for far too long. This is our chance to make things right for our family."

Duke returns without the ball and growls at my father. It's low and rough, from somewhere deep down in his throat.

"I'd let me go if I were you," I say softly, cocking a brow and looking my father in the eye. Duke doesn't have the type of control I do. But he'll always wait for my command.

"What, you gonna send that fucking dog after me?" He scoffs, but it's quick and panic is barely hidden beneath it.

"No," I say, staring him down. "You know I don't need his help."

There's a strained moment between us. I can see my father doing the math in his head, wondering if he could take me in a fair fight now that I'm older. We've come close to fighting in the past, though we've never actually traded blows. But we both know I have youth and experience on my side, and so he slowly releases me and takes a deep breath.

He picks up the cigar he dropped on the ground and takes a long puff, looking away as he walks back to the oak tree, ignoring everything that just happened. That's what he does. Thickheaded, thin-skinned and hot-tempered. That's the Romano in him.

I walk across the yard and bend down, picking up the ball Duke left, and throw it. Duke darts after it as if nothing happened.

"Just think about it," he finally says, forcing me to look over my shoulder and face him. "If we kill this fucker, we can be rolling in it for a long time."

"If we kill this fucker, we can start a war." I bite out my words. That's the real reason I don't want in on this.

He shrugs, rubbing out his cigar on the tree and letting out a deep exhalation of smoke. "Let's just wait and see what they have to say." He glances at me, a look of determination on his face, and then heads off back toward his truck.

I don't watch him go. I know he's pissed, and I understand that. Fuck, I can't even blame him, not really. Joining the *familia* is his lifelong dream, and if someone got in the way of what I wanted, well, I'd fucking kill them.

Too bad the old bastard needs me. The sound of his truck starting fills the chilly air as Duke comes back to me.

I'm his rightful successor. He's getting old, too old to go on hits, and for the last two years I've been taking on more and more of the load. In fact, he hasn't actually killed in nearly six months, which is strange for a man who makes his living in death.

He raised me to be a killer and to be the fucking best at what I do. From a young age I remember going to shooting ranges, and practicing knife skills. My childhood was almost exclusively learning to fight, learning to stalk, and learning how to kill efficiently and quietly. My father trained me to be a hitman, and I quickly found out that I was damn good at it.

And I like it. I like tracking down my victims and taking their lives. They all deserve it. They have it coming to them. As far as I'm concerned, I'm doing the world a favor. I like the power and respect I get for being a skilled and in-demand assassin. Nobody fucks with me because they know who I am, and what I'm capable of. No one can push me around. They wouldn't fucking dare.

But I can't deny that it fucked me up. That it changed me. I can remember the way I was back when I was still a kid, back before killing became my life. The darkness wasn't there back then. I wasn't born with it. It was created.

As I pitch the ball across the yard again, I remember the day my father brought me completely into this life and forced me to kill a man for the first time.

My father stands over me in the cellar. My breath comes in ragged, short gasps.

"Don't be a pussy," he says to me, his voice barely above a whisper as he grips my shoulders. "You fucking afraid?"

"No," I say, but I'm lying. I'm terrified. I'm ten years old and I've never seen a man die before. Not in real life.

The old man's tied to a chair with a gag in his mouth, muffling his screams and pleas. I don't know him. His eyes are wide and brown. His hair is receding and he's probably fifty years old, but I didn't really know that back then. I was just a kid. I didn't know anything.

"What did he do?" I ask tentatively, and my voice cracks. My heart is beating so loudly I can hardly hear anything else.

My father whirls on me. "You fucking know not to ask questions." The anger in his voice makes me flinch. Ever since Mom died, it's been different between us. He takes his rage out on me. It's my fault.

"I know," I say, looking away from him. I expect him to hit me, and I wait for it… but he doesn't. My body is so hot. I feel like I can't even breathe.

"It doesn't matter what he did. All that matters is we get paid. These guys, they're all shit. You have to understand that." The man screams again behind his gag, but whatever he's saying is dampened. I wish I knew.

"I understand." I look at the man as my father walks over to him. He takes the man by what hair he has left and pulls his head back.

"Look at him, Gio," my father says. "Look at this man. Are you looking?"

"Yes, father," I say, staring at the man.

"This is our prey. He's our victim. He's nothing." My father releases him. "Are you a fucking pussy?"

"No," I say and step toward the man. My nerves are shaken, but I have to do this.

"Good. Very good, Gio."

The man struggles and tries to say something. He's panicking and trying to move again like he knows it's his last chance. My father backhands him across the face and his head droops. He's dazed, but not unconscious.

"What now?" I ask my father. I've been training for this since I was very young. I know how to shoot and how to fight and how to hunt, but this is the first time my father is making me watch.

Except watching isn't what he has planned. He holds his gun out to me, grip first. "Take it," he says.

I stare at him, shocked. "Why?" I ask.

"Do as I say."

Afraid, I take the gun. I expect him to hit me again for not following orders right away, but he doesn't. My hands shake.

I know something irreversible is happening. But I don't understand what, not yet.

"Press it against his head," my father orders.

I stand so close to the man I can feel the heat and desperation roiling off of him. His eyes are wide and pleading, staring at me, practically looking through me. He squirms against the restraints. I press the gun against his head. My throat is so tight, I can't swallow. I watch as the man begins to cry, deep heaving sobs. I hold the gun there, the cold steel feeling hotter as my hand starts to sweat, and I look at my father.

"Look back at him," my father commands. I try to swallow again, but I fail miserably. I stare at the man, but only at his temple where the gun is pointed. I can't look him in the eyes. "Are you ready, Gio?"

It comes to me in that moment, what my father wants. It's the reason he's not hitting me. Because he knows I'm about to do something important. I don't want to though. I don't want this. I hold the gun tightly, then grip it with two hands.

"I- I-" I stammer. I can't do this. I'm not like him.

"You will do it, or I'll untie him and let him beat you to death," my father sneers. My blood runs cold, and I finally swallow the spiked lump that has formed in my throat.

"I'm ready," I say in a voice I don't recognize.

Ten years old. My father puts a hand on my shoulder. His fingers dig in as he squeezes.

"Do it," he says.

I pull the trigger without thinking anything more. Bang! The man's skull explodes in a shower of blood. The sound, the feel, and the sight of the man, hung over and limp in the chair haunted me for years. But not the next man, or the next that my father had me kill. I don't even remember them.

I HATE HIM FOR WHAT HE MADE ME, BUT AT THE SAME time, I'm also glad for what he made me. I can take lives so easily now. They mean nothing to me. That first time was difficult, but it was also surprisingly easy.

One pull of the trigger, and it all ends. I'm safe, and the world is rid of a man who needed to die. The darkness inside of me needs this. It craves the rush and the thrill of a hunt and a kill, and if I go too long without a job I find that darkness coming up to the surface in the form of memories. Too much of my past still haunts me. I just need to focus on the present. *On the next kill.*

Duke returns with the ball. I crouch down and pat his shoulder, just now noticing how the sky has darkened and the air has turned bitter cold. "Good boy," I say softly. I relax as Duke nudges me, bringing me back to the present. "Next time, just rip off his nuts."

Duke licks my hand as I grin, pick up the ball, and throw it. He barks as he runs off, leaving me alone with the dilemma at hand.

My father wants me to at least hear what they have to say, and I can do that. I'll listen, because I owe him that much. But I can't imagine how they could change my mind on this one. Not when this hit could spark the largest mafia war in the history of the whole fucking city.

Grace

Knock, knock. The hard pounding on my bedroom door forces my eyes open. I don't shake or shudder, and I don't flinch when the door opens without a response from me. I'm used to it now. My breathing comes in carefully, each movement calculated.

The door creaks and then shuts with a loud bang as I rise and blink the sleep from my eyes. I don't know how long I've been asleep, but it doesn't matter. It's not like I have anything else to do, or anywhere to go.

I restrain myself from stretching and sit up on the edge of my bed, my hands clasped in my lap as I watch my father walk toward me. I'm used to this, but my heart still races with fear. Everything else I can control, but not my heart. No matter how much I want it to remain calm, it always beats harder and tries to escape up my throat whenever he comes to get me. I never know what to expect, but I know how to behave. I've learned the hard way, but now I know how to survive. That's all I do… *survive*.

If I was a boy, it wouldn't be like this. But I'm a *disappointment*. A reminder of my mother, and how she betrayed him. That's all I am. He never fails to make sure I know it.

"You need to do something for me," he says in a lowered voice. It holds the edge of a threat when he talks to me. It's always there, like he's waiting for me to give him a reason to strike me. Unless Uncle Toni's in the room. Just the thought of my godfather makes my heart calm slightly. He can't kill me with my uncle still around. My mother, yes, but not me. Uncle Toni would never allow it.

My father may be the Don of the Rossi *familia*, but everyone knows my uncle Toni calls the shots. They all look to him with respect, and they're loyal to him… not to my father. The very thought almost wills me to smile, but I'm not that foolish.

"The Romanos are up to something." I stare straight ahead, my neck stiff as he talks.

He crosses the room, moving to my window and then back toward me. "They've been circling our territory and looking for something." He continues talking without waiting for a response. He doesn't need one from me. We both know that.

I bow my head and keep my eyes down as he paces the floor in front of me. His suit pants swish as he walks and make up the only background noise. He usually doesn't talk *business* around me. He says it's not for women, and I honestly prefer to be left out of it. My fingers dig into the comforter as he speaks, knowing something terrible is going to happen. I don't want to know, but for him to be telling me these things… it's not good. "I don't like it, and you're going to fix this," he practically hisses, turning harshly in his spot and staring at me. I look up to meet his gaze, but only to keep him from touching me. My eyes meet his as I nod my head like I'm supposed to, but inside I'm screaming.

"The Romanos have been hanging around our restaurant; they're on our turf, looking for trouble." His pale blue eyes piercing into mine hold me hostage as my lungs pause their movements. "You're going out there as bait."

I don't react, but he still holds up his pointer and lowers his voice as if I've disobeyed him. Sometimes I can't prevent him from beating me, but it's best not to react, so I'm still as he says, "You don't have a choice. You're going to get us the information we need, and we'll get you out."

For a moment I question if he'll really come save me, or if the Romanos will get to keep me. I'm not sure it matters much. Although at least here I know what to expect. I rely on the comfort of familiarity. I search my father's face for answers, for reassurance. But there's nothing there. Only emptiness in his dark eyes.

"They're going to take you. You need to trust me and stay focused. Listen to what they say and when I come to get you, you'll tell me everything."

I'm numb to his words. It wouldn't be the first time he's used me for his own plans. I nod my head once, although I don't speak. He doesn't like it when I talk.

My heart leaps in my chest as he grips my chin in his hand and rips my head to the side.

"Answer me!" he screams at me. His stale breath fills my lungs as I heave in a frightened breath. After all these years I still cower. Maybe there's a part of me that isn't dead yet.

"Yes, father. I'll listen to everything." My throat feels so tight, but the words come out calmly. "I'll tell you everything." My blood runs cold. I ignore the voices arguing inside of me. One is telling me to run, and the other is telling me to fight back. Those voices are useless. *They both get me nothing but beatings.* I'm smarter than that now. It's not about fear, only survival.

"Good," he says as he releases me, and I fall back into place as he talks to me. "We'll drop you off at the restaurant, and you can walk back home. They've been scouting every day in the evening, so it shouldn't take more than a day or two before they get confident and take you."

I half expect him to tell me not to worry, but I don't hold my breath. I should be worried, and I am. More than that, he doesn't give a fuck if I live or die. Maybe he really needs the information, or maybe he's just looking to finally get rid of me.

I think about what he's asking, and hope rises in my chest.

I'll be alone. For the first time since I can remember, I'll be alone. I try to hide the excitement rising in me. *The hope.*

Maybe this will be my chance to run. I don't want to be the Rossi mafia princess anymore. I don't want to be a pawn in my father's games and get married off to whoever he wants to make alliances with. Although there's a faint hope that I can run and disappear, it's only barely there. It's faded to a mere whisper of what it used to be.

I've tried before to run, and failed. I have the scars to prove it's not possible to outrun the Rossis.

"Do you understand, Grace?" my father asks, practically spitting out my name like a curse.

"Yes, father." My eyes fall to the floor. It's better not to look him in the eyes, especially when I feel like this… when I feel hopeful. "Whatever you need me to do."

"Good." He turns and walks to the door with heavy steps, speaking without looking at me. "Get yourself dressed. We're leaving soon."

My hands ball into fists as the door closes, and my breathing comes in ragged pants. The facade leaves me quickly. I hate him. With everything in my being, I hate him. I rise from the bed and look out my window. It's nailed shut from the outside to keep me from jumping.

Outside, it's dark and grey with clouds covering nearly every inch of the visible sky. It reflects everything that I feel.

I walk to my dresser, my eyes darting to the door. Inside the top drawer, I dig under the pile of shirts and pick up a small bag of heroin. I wrap my fingers around it tightly. I've never done the drug, or any others for that matter. I stole it. I've collected a few baggies over time, and I know I have enough to easily overdose now.

I've been thinking about suicide for a while, but I haven't had the courage to end it. I don't want to die; I just don't want to live *this* life anymore. There's a difference. I stare at the heroin, feeling every emotion wash over me. I knew one day I'd need it.

I would be a fool not to take the heroin with me. I need a way out in case my father doesn't come for me and leaves me there. In case that fate is worse than this. I open the drawer containing my underwear and select my favorite push-up bra. Quickly, I slide the packet into one of the pockets containing the padded inserts. I just hope that whoever takes me won't search my clothing too closely, but in my experience the perverts I've been exposed to care more about seeing a woman naked than her lingerie.

But hopefully it won't even come close to that. He's

giving me a chance to run. An opportunity I've prayed for.

Maybe God was listening. Maybe I'll be free soon.

If not, if I can't get away from my father, if I can't get away from the Romanos… at least I'll have a way out.

Click here to keep reading Forsaken!